Finding Grace

A Gutsy Girl Book

Finding Grace

Becky Citra

Second Story Press

Library and Archives Canada Cataloguing in Publication

Citra, Becky, author
Finding Grace / by Becky Citra.

(The gutsy girl series)
Issued in print and electronic formats.
ISBN 978-1-927583-25-8 (pbk.). —ISBN 978-1-927583-26-5 (epub)

I. Title. II. Series: Gutsy girl book

PS8555 I87 F55 2014   jC813'.54   C2014-900600-4

C2014-900601-2

Cover by Gillian Newland
Edited by Gena Gorrell and Kya McMillan
Designed by Melissa Kaita

Printed and bound in Canada

*Second Story Press gratefully acknowledges the support of the Ontario Arts Council
and the Canada Council for the Arts for our publishing program. We acknowledge
the financial support of the Government of Canada through the Canada Book Fund.*

Canada Council   Conseil des Arts
for the Arts   du Canada

MIX
Paper from
responsible sources
FSC® C004071

Published by
SECOND STORY PRESS
20 Maud Street, Suite 401
Toronto, ON M5V 2M5
www.secondstorypress.ca

For Bev

Part One

VANCOUVER, 1954

Chapter One

Dear Grace,

I have been accused of a crime! Someone stole Nancy Collier's brand-new glow-in-the-dark yo-yo today. Miss Noonan did a desk check. I wasn't worried (why would I be?), but guess where the yo-yo turned up? In MY desk! Sweartogod I didn't take it. Miss Noonan made me stay in at recess and lunch, but I refused to confess. I'm innocent!

Mom didn't get out of bed all day. She pretended she did, but I can tell. She was in her nightie when I got home, and her hair was smushed on one side and she smelled sour, like sweaty running shoes. That means she will want to stay up all night, and she'll make me watch TV with her and I'll be tired again at school tomorrow.

She just called me to bring her a cup of coffee.

"You got a broken leg?" I yelled back.

But I better go. I'll write some more later.

Your best friend,

Hope

Mom hates Grace. That's why I have to hide these letters in a shoebox in my cupboard. I think I was about three years old when I made Grace up. When I started kindergarten, Mom said I had to stop talking about Grace. She said imaginary friends were for little kids, and that everyone would think I was weird. I remember her slapping my hand when I set three places at the table and poured an extra glass of milk. Then she started yelling at me if I even said the name.

After that, I went underground with Grace.

When I'm feeling sad or worried, I write to Grace every day. Then I forget about her for weeks and weeks. I think I'm what Granny calls a fair-weather friend.

Right now I'm smack in the middle of a bad stretch. Really bad. This is why:

Mom hasn't been to her job at the dry cleaners for exactly twenty-seven days. I'm pretty sure we're running out of money *fast*. Proof: I eat almost all my meals at Granny's, and she makes my lunch for school every day. That's not as inconvenient as it sounds, because she lives in an apartment one floor below us. Granny makes these weirdly amazing soups, like peanut butter and onion. Mom won't touch them. As far as I can figure out, she only eats crackers and tomato soup from a can.

I wish I knew what was wrong with her, but I don't. I wish I knew what to do.

Chapter Two

We're doing family trees at school. So far I have three names:

Me: Hope Rose King
Mom: Flora Rosalie King
Granny: Lillian Janet King

I suck the end of my pencil and pretend to be thinking. The girl who sits beside me, Lesley Thomas, is writing furiously. She leans back in her chair and says, "Eighteen cousins! Phew!"

How could anyone have eighteen cousins???

"I don't give a darn," I tell her. I stop myself from rolling my eyes just in time. I'm trying very hard to make a best friend at this school.

"Whoops, nineteen." She glances sideways at me. "I forgot Oliver."

I slide my arm around my paper so she can't see it.

The girl behind me (that nasty Barbara Porter) puts up her hand and asks, "Can we include great-great-grandparents?"

Who even *knows* about great-great-grandparents? Granny must have had parents and grandparents, but I have no clue who they were. She had a husband who's dead. I know she has no brothers or sisters. We're a family of only children: Granny, and then Mom, and now me.

When class started, kids pulled out scraps of paper covered with names, and I remembered too late that we were supposed to interview our parents and grandparents last night.

I glance around the room. I'm the only one who isn't writing. Lesley is coloring her family tree now. Purple for her nineteen cousins. Her paper has lines going everywhere, like a giant rainbow spider web.

"Be creative," Miss Noonan says. She holds up Mark's paper – he has drawn an actual tree with leaves.

Miss Noonan is floating between the desks. She wears short, brightly colored dresses – a different one every day of the week – and she smells like strawberries. Half the girls in the class have a crush on her. Probably all the boys, too.

"You can have the rest of the afternoon to work on these," she says.

I peek at the clock. Forty-five minutes until bell time. What I really want to do is put my head down and sleep.

I know you can fail math tests (I've failed seven and I'm in serious danger of failing grade five), but can you fail family trees?

I decide to give Granny some parents. I draw two spokes coming out of her name. At the end of one I print *Mortimer Noah King*. On the other one I print *Joelle Hyacinth King*.

I give Granny a sister, Camilla Dominique King, and a brother, Chadwick Lucas King.

Mom gets four sisters and a brother. Presto! I now have aunts and an uncle.

I give Mom a husband (which she never had) who is also my father (whom I've never known). I spend some time on his name and come up with *Nigel Nicholas King*.

I'd love to give myself a sister. I would call her a beautiful name, like Jacqueline, but then everyone would wonder where she is. Instead, I work on giving my aunts and my uncle lots of kids.

When the bell rings, I put my pencil down. Lesley is staring at me.

"Twenty cousins," I say. "Beat that."

Dear Grace,

Miss Noonan handed back the family trees today. Everyone got a mark except me. I got "*See me.*" I stayed behind at recess.

"Something is puzzling me," Miss Noonan said. "Everyone in your extended family has the same last name, King."

Oops. I should have thought of that. I should have invented some different last names, like Montgomery (my favorite author).

I've only been at this school for three months and I really want Miss Noonan to like me. Now she thinks I'm a cheater and a thief (I am still the chief suspect in the stolen yo-yo mystery). All the kids will think so too, and I'll *never* have any friends except for you.

Your best friend,
Hope

Chapter Three

"I humiliated myself in front of Miss Noonan," I tell Mom. "Couldn't you at least tell me my father's name?"

Mom, Granny, and I are the only ones on a bus going downtown, so we can have this conversation without anyone listening in.

Granny says snarkily, "Wouldn't we all like to know?"

Mom lowers her sunglasses and narrows her eyes at her. Then she turns to me. "Do you do this on purpose to upset me?" she asks me.

What did Granny mean? Did my mother have so many boyfriends that she doesn't *know* who my father is?

"I can't talk about this right now," Mom snaps.

Up until now, I've been sort of enjoying myself. The

three of us are on a mission to buy me some new clothes for the summer. Well, not exactly new. That's why I said *sort of*. We're going to a thrift shop.

Let one thing be clear: I have never worn used clothes before. This is further proof that we are running out of money.

The best part of today is that it's bright and sunny outside and Mom is outdoors. She squinted when she came out of the apartment building, like a lizard that has been under a rock too long. Then she put on sunglasses to hide her puffy eyes. She has lipstick and blusher on and is wearing a dress with sunflowers on it and white sandals. She looks gorgeous, like a movie star.

Granny knows two thrift shops in our part of the city. One is near our apartment building, but it's too near my school. A fate worse than death would be to show up at school in nasty Barbara Porter's old dress. So I make Mom take me to the other shop, which means we have to ride the bus.

The thrift shop is in a green building beside a Laundromat. Outside the door there are two huge bins for donations. They're full of toys, a kitchen chair missing rungs, a small record player, and a scruffy-looking fur coat.

Inside, at the front, is a long counter. A woman is sorting clothes into piles. She glances up and says, "Good afternoon."

"Good afternoon," Mom says.

"Do you wash these clothes before you put them out on the racks?" I ask. Mom gives me a dirty look and Granny jabs me with a sharp elbow. The woman ignores me.

I look around. Clothes are lined up on hangers, in rows labeled with signs that read *jackets, women's blouses,* and *suits.* I poke through the girls' sections. I find a pair of pale yellow pants that look brand-new, a blue top with white polka dots, and some plain brown shorts. Finding a dress takes longer, but I finally settle on a cute green shirtdress with a white belt.

I try on everything behind a curtain in the corner of the store. It all fits. I check each item carefully for rips or stains, but don't find any. I have to wait ages while Mom and Granny try on piles of clothes. Then Mom says suddenly that she's exhausted and has to go home. Granny says, "Don't let *me* hold you up," and neither of them buys anything.

When we get out to the sidewalk, a voice calls, "Hello, Flora."

Flora is my mother. We all spin around. A tall man in a dark suit and a gray hat is smiling at us. "Nice to see you're feeling better," he says. "We've missed you at work."

Mom turns bright red – like a tomato.

She nods and mumbles something about coming back

on Monday. Then she herds Granny and me toward the bus stop.

"Is he my long-lost father?" I whisper.

"*Hope!*" Mom says.

"*Just kidding!*"

Mom peers behind her to make sure the man is gone. "That's Mr. Finlater. He owns the dry-cleaning shop where I work."

Granny notices Mom blushing too. "He has a wedding ring," she points out. "That probably means he has a *wife*."

That's what Mom calls one of Granny's cheap shots. And it isn't fair. Anyone with half a brain can tell that Mom isn't blushing because she likes Mr. Finlater. She's blushing because he caught her out shopping when she's supposed to be sick. Besides, she doesn't fall all over men. She's just so pretty that they want to go out with her. I can count back at least five boyfriends. The last one, Calvin, was the best. He brought chocolates – Mom shared – and flowers and Chanel Number 5 perfume that Mom let me try.

The night Mom broke it off (she always breaks up with her boyfriends, not the other way around), I found her in her bed, crying. "I'm a terrible person," she wailed. "I don't deserve to be happy."

I don't think she was talking about breaking Calvin's heart. I think she meant something else.

The truth is, I have always known that Mom has some deep, dark secret. But I don't have the foggiest idea what it is.

Right now Mom is boyfriendless. Mr. Finlater is handsome, but he is too old for her. And yes, he probably has a wife.

The bus wheezes to a stop in front of us and the door swings open. Mom goes first. "Putting up with the two of you," she says over her shoulder, "it's no wonder I'm crazy."

Dear Grace,

Do you think Mom really could be crazy?

I have never considered that possibility before. I think of her as just terribly, terribly sad. So sad that sometimes she won't get out of bed.

Frightened.

Worried.

Sometimes mad at me for no reason.

But crazy? I don't want her to end up in a mental institution.

Your best friend,
Hope

P.S. Do you think the chemicals at the dry-cleaning shop have done something to her brain?

•••••

Dear Grace,

Good news! Nancy Collier confessed that SHE hid her yo-yo in my desk! So no one stole it after all! Miss Noonan apologized to me, and said that sometimes people who are very unhappy do peculiar things for attention.

I don't feel sorry for Nancy. She may be unhappy, but she can't have half the problems I have. I also have to admit that in a crazy way, I was starting to enjoy my situation. At least I had a certain kind of notoriety.

Your best friend,
Hope

Chapter Four

Mom went to work this morning, but she's home in her nightie when I get back from school.

"Mr. Finlater gave my job to someone else," she says.

"*What?*" I remember how he smiled at Mom in front of the thrift shop. "The creep! How could he?"

Mom shrugs. "Anyway, I can't afford the rent anymore. We're going to have to move."

"Again?"

Before coming here, we lived in the basement of someone's house, and before that, in half of a duplex. Each time we moved, it was to a different part of the city and I had to change schools. We moved into this apartment three months ago. Granny has been living in this building for twenty years, since my grandfather died. When a rental became available upstairs, Mom hemmed and hawed and said she wasn't sure. Granny said, "Don't look a gift horse in the mouth, Flora. It's a good neighborhood, and I can help keep an eye on Hope."

And now we have to move again.

Mom gives me a tired smile. "Not so far this time. Just downstairs with Granny."

Granny's apartment is cluttered with spindly chairs and little tables and tons of fragile ornaments you're not even allowed to breathe on. "How will there be room for us?" I ask.

"We'll put most of our stuff in boxes," Mom says. "There's lots of storage space in the basement."

I try to imagine us squeezed in with Granny. Her apartment is the same layout as ours: kitchen, living room, two bedrooms, and one bathroom.

Wait a sec. *Two bedrooms.*

"So you and Granny are going to share a bedroom?"

"That's impossible," Mom says. "I need my own room."

"I need my own room too!"

"I'm sorry. The couch in the living room makes into a bed. That will have to do for you for a while. Until I get another job and we can afford our own place again."

"The living room? I'm going to sleep in Granny's living

room?" I'm shouting, but I can't help it. "I need *privacy*. Where am I supposed to get dressed?"

"The bathroom?" Mom closes her eyes. "Don't do this to me, Hope. I'm going to lie down." She disappears into her bedroom.

I slam a few doors to make my point. Then I go downstairs to Granny's. Her cat, Jingle, is lying in a patch of sun on the kitchen floor, glaring at me through slitted eyes.

"It's not fair," I tell Granny.

She looks up from the pot of beet borscht she's stirring. "Life isn't fair, chicklet," she says. "Now come and taste this for me."

Borscht is my absolute favorite soup, and I'm pretty sure she's making it specially for me.

Chapter Five

It's moving day.

Mom stands in the doorway of my bedroom, her hands folded across her chest. "You can't take your books. There's no room. We'll have to put them in storage."

She can't be serious.

"I need them," I say.

"But you've read them all." She's trying to be patient, but a muscle in her cheek is twitching.

"I might want to read them again."

"Three. The rest go in the basement."

This is agony. I have exactly twenty-seven books. Books are mostly all I ask for at Christmas and on my birthday. I keep changing my mind, but finally I decide on *The Wind in the Willows, The Lion, the Witch and the Wardrobe,* and *Jane of Lantern Hill* (my all-time favorite – Jane lives with her mother and grandmother too, and suffers almost as much as I do).

The rest of my packing is easy: winter clothes and my ice skates go into three cardboard cartons for storage, and summer clothes go into a couple of laundry baskets. My jacks, my bag of marbles, my Slinky, my writing paper and pens, my skipping rope, and my stuffed hippo, Harry, all go in a shopping bag.

I hide my Dear Grace letters in one of the laundry baskets, under a pile of tops.

The furniture belongs with the apartment. We store our dishes and pots and pans in boxes since Granny has enough stuff for all of us. Mom has arranged for the landlord's son to move all the boxes into the basement.

I take lots of trips in the elevator to Granny's apartment, dragging the laundry baskets, my shopping bag, and blankets and pillows. I pile everything in the middle of Granny's living room, between the rickety tables and chairs.

"Be careful you don't break anything, sweetie," Granny says. She's watching me from her recliner, with Jingle in her lap. He's old, maybe even ancient. Granny got him before I was born and she says he wasn't a young cat then. She says the reason he has lived so long is that he's an inside cat and doesn't have to fend off dogs and cars. He has long, thick, black and gold fur and he may be part Persian. He likes to leap out and scratch your legs when you're not looking. He really only likes Granny.

She's smoking, and a gray haze surrounds her. She never opens windows. She hates drafts. I pretend to cough like crazy, "UGHGHG! UGHGHG! UGHGHG!" but she doesn't get the hint.

When everything is moved, we have meatloaf, peas, and strawberry ice cream for supper.

Mom plays with her food. "Why do I always have such rotten luck?" she says.

"You make your bed, you have to lie in it," Granny tells her.

Granny isn't really mean. She must hate having us all crammed in here together. And she's mad that Mom doesn't even try to get a job. I heard them arguing last week and Mom yelled, "You know why. *You know why!*" I just wish I knew why, but no one tells me anything.

I've never slept in a living room before. It doesn't get completely dark because there's a streetlight right outside the window, shining through the lacy curtains. The mattress on the pull-out couch is as thin as cardboard, and metal pieces stab my back. I'm trying to pretend that this is a pajama party (I've never been to a pajama party, but I've heard girls talk about them), but it doesn't work because I'm the only one here.

I turn on the light, put my hippo, Harry, beside me, and read *Jane of Lantern Hill* for a while. Jane's grandmother is plain evil and I take back what I said about Jane suffering almost as much as me. She suffers *much* more. I feel a little bit better.

Until I get up to go to the bathroom.

That's when I hear Mom, behind her bedroom door.

She's crying.

•••••

Dear Grace,

We've been living in Granny's apartment for two weeks. I can only write when Mom's in bed because I have no privacy here, and she'll freak out if she finds out about these letters.

Tonight I leaned across a little table and the sleeve of my dressing gown knocked a china figurine onto the floor. It was a ROYAL DOULTON figurine and they cost a fortune!!!!! It was one of Granny's favorites, of a little boy and a puppy. It smashed to smithereens.

"No use crying over spilt milk," Granny said.

"It was my fault for putting it on the table and not in the cabinet with the others." But she didn't want to play Chinese checkers with me before bed. Proof she is mad: we ALWAYS play Chinese checkers.

Mom finally went to a job interview yesterday, to be a clerk at a grocery store. She curled her hair and wore high heels and Granny said she looked like a million dollars. But she didn't get the job.

I read the sad part in *Jane of Lantern Hill* today, when she has to leave her dad and Prince Edward Island and go back to her grandmother's house in Toronto. I cried buckets.

Your best friend,
Hope

P.S. Miss Noonan told us that she read an article in the newspaper about cigarettes maybe causing cancer, and said she hopes none of us ever starts to smoke. Do you think that could be true? Granny smokes like a chimney. Cancer! What would we do without Granny? One more thing for me to worry about.

Chapter Six

"This," Mom says, after we've had supper one night, "is a picture of your father."

I'm sitting at the dining room table, in the alcove between the kitchen and the living room, sweating over math. The problems are horrible and don't make sense. I'm petrified all over again about failing grade five.

Granny is in her armchair, knitting a pair of purple socks for me.

Mom has been drifting in and out of the room for the last hour, reading a magazine for a few minutes, switching the TV on and off.

She puts a small square photograph on the table in front of me. "You're old enough to see this."

My heart beats faster as I study the black-and-white picture. It's of four young men in uniform, standing in front of a train.

"The one on the right," Mom says. "His name was Tommy."

"Tommy *who?*" I say.

She sighs. "I don't think I ever knew."

"Where did you meet him?"

"A dance."

The photograph is blurry and I can't tell exactly what he looks like, but I can see that he's grinning.

A soldier!

"Was he devastatingly handsome?" I ask hopefully.

"No," Mom says. "He was actually quite ordinary."

Ordinary. Like me. I definitely don't look like Mom. I have straight brown hair (Mom's is curly and a nicer brown than mine), brown eyes (Mom's are sky blue), my chin is square, and I hate to admit it, but my nose is a bit too big for my face (Mom's is perfectly dainty). I am also as skinny as a stick, but my feet are fat. Mom is curvy, but I am all straight lines and bones. My looks must have come from my father, but the photograph is not much help.

"Why didn't you marry him?"

"It wasn't like that. I only knew him for a week."

Granny's knitting needles click furiously.

"So what happened?"

"He went to war."

I stare some more at the photograph. None of the soldiers look very old.

"Didn't he come to see you when he came back?"

"He didn't come back."

Holy Toledo! A thrill runs up my spine. "He was shot down by enemy fire," I breathe.

"Food poisoning," Mom says. "I heard that he ate some fish that wasn't canned properly." She adds, "You can have the picture. I don't want it."

"Thank you," I say.

It's a very disappointing story. But it's all I have.

Chapter Seven

We're having a Strawberry Tea at school. It's just for grade five mothers and daughters. The boys grumble a bit when Miss Noonan says they're not invited, but I don't think they really want to come.

I do. I can't wait. None of the girls at school have seen my mother yet. I'm going to ask Granny to curl Mom's hair again the way she did for the job interview. I hope Mom wears makeup and her dress with the sunflowers.

I have never been to a Strawberry Tea. This is how it works: the boys will go home at three o'clock and the girls will stay. The tea will be in the gym – strawberry shortcake and tea in real china teacups. We'll sit at card tables with our mothers and some of the girls in grade six will serve us.

Then we'll sing a song about robins and recite some mushy poems that we have been practicing.

In Art today, the girls make invitations while the boys draw anything they want. I draw a bright red strawberry on the front of mine. On the inside, I copy the information carefully from the blackboard:

Come to our Mother Daughter Strawberry Tea!
Queens Elementary School
June 6, 3:30 p.m.

I take the invitation home and Mom puts it on a table in the living room.

"I wouldn't miss it for the world," she says.

• • • • •

On the afternoon of the tea, I ask Miss Noonan three times if I can go to the bathroom. I don't really have to go, I just want to peek in the gym. It looks elegant. The card tables are covered with white paper, folded over and taped at the corners. On each table are cups and saucers, tiny yellow napkins, and a jar filled with blue flowers. There are also little cards with our names and our mothers' names on them, printed in Miss Noonan's calligraphy.

At first I felt sick to see that nasty Barbara Porter and her mother are sitting with Mom and me. But I've seen Mrs. Porter pick Barbara up after school, and she is quite honestly not at all pretty like my mom, so I've calmed down about it.

Everyone is so excited that at two-thirty Miss Noonan gives up and sends the boys outside to play baseball, while we girls brush our hair, check our dresses in the long mirror by the door, and talk about our mothers.

I'll admit it. I brag a little. "My mother used to be a model," I say.

"Right," Barbara says snarkily.

"It's true. Her picture was in the newspaper. Lots."

"Prove it," Fiona says.

"I will. I'll bring some pictures."

Granny has a scrapbook full of pictures of Mom from the *Vancouver Province*. Mom was modeling spring and fall clothes – dresses, hats, even a ball gown – for the fashion supplement. She was eighteen years old and she hadn't had me yet. She looked ravishing.

The bell rings. We practice our song and poems one last time and head to the gym. Mothers in their flowery summer dresses are already filling the hallway. I peer around anxiously for mine. She isn't here yet, but it's only twenty after three. My mom is never early for anything.

Miss Noonan herds everyone into the gym and we find our tables. Miss Noonan has made us practice making introductions, and Barbara introduces me to her mother without making any mistakes. "Mother, this is Hope King. Hope, this is my mother, Mrs. Porter."

I smile and shake hands but my eyes keep flitting to the door. Mom should be here by now. Where *is* she?

A grade six girl brings around a teapot and pours our tea, and another girl brings a tray with plates of strawberry shortcake. It looks utterly scrumptious and I take a forkful but I can barely swallow. Sweat trickles down my back. *Where is she?*

Mrs. Porter chatters about how lovely everything looks and how she's really looking forward to the entertainment. "Barbara's been practicing in her room, but she won't let me listen."

Barbara gives her mother a blank stare. Then she says, between mouthfuls, "Where's *your* mother?"

I glance around and I almost faint. Granny is standing by the door. Even from here, I can tell that she is dressed all wrong. She's wearing her hot pink wool suit that's ten years old, and around her neck is a real fur stole that my grandfather gave her when they got married.

Her hair is, well, orange.

This morning when I left for school it was a normal

brown, but she's been talking about dying it for ages. Cripes. Why did she have to pick today?

Miss Noonan intercepts her and brings her over to our table. I realize, in a sudden panic, that she may introduce Granny as my mother. Miss Noonan has never met my mother, and Granny is old – sixty – but not *really* old.

I say quickly, "Hi, Granny," and Mrs. Porter says smoothly, "What a lovely idea to invite your grandmother," as if I have done this on purpose.

Up close, you can see that Granny has put on too much powder and that her red lipstick is crooked, and this is not a nice thing to think, but she reeks of cigarette smoke.

Barbara's mouth hangs open.

The tea passes in a blur. Granny and Mrs. Porter hit it off and talk about all kinds of things. Barbara and I don't say a word to each other.

During the entertainment, Granny claps like crazy. People are staring at her. I pretend she's not related to me.

When it's all over and we're walking home, she keeps saying what a wonderful time she had. I half listen while I plan what I'm going to say to my mother. By the time we get back to the apartment, I'm ready to explode.

Mom is hiding in her room. *The coward.*

I kick her closed door.

Hard.

Dear Grace,

At the Strawberry Tea today I went to the bathroom and I was in a cubicle just finishing when two girls came in. I pulled my legs up on the toilet and held my breath so they wouldn't know I was there.

I recognized Lesley Thomas's shoes. They have bows on them. "Is that Hope's *MOTHER*?" she said. (That is exactly how she said it.)

"I thought she was supposed to be a model," added a girl who sounded like Lesley's best friend, Betty Walker.

"She's awfully old, anyway," Lesley said. "And weird."

I slammed my feet down and marched out of the cubicle. Lesley and Betty gaped at me. "That was my *grand*mother. Not that it's any of your beeswax," I said with as much dignity as I could muster.

It shut them up, but it didn't feel great.

How am I ever going to face everyone tomorrow?

Your best friend,
Hope

P.S. Granny won't even let me take the modeling scrapbook to school. *Nobody* is on my side!

Chapter Eight

A few days later, just before the last bell, the principal, Mr. Hubert, comes to our classroom. He talks in a low voice to Miss Noonan, who is sitting at her desk marking exercise books while the class copies a poem off the blackboard.

They both look at me. I can't think of anything that I have done wrong, but my cheeks burn. I slide my eyes around the room. A lot of kids are staring at me.

Mr. Hubert leaves and Miss Noonan calls me up to her desk. "Your grandmother's been taken to Vancouver General Hospital," she says. "You're supposed to meet your mother there after school."

My heart leaps into my throat. Questions fire out of me. "What do you mean? What's wrong? What happened?"

"Take a big breath, Hope," Miss Noonan says. "Try not to always overreact to everything. I'm sure she'll be fine."

Easy for her to say. It's not *her* granny.

"How will I get there?"

"Your mother wants you to take the bus. She said you're good with buses. It's not very far."

Miss Noonan starts writing instructions on a piece of paper, but she must be able to tell that I'm not taking any of it in because she finally sighs and says, "I'll drive you."

· · · · ·

A bunch of kids, including nasty Barbara Porter, stand around while I'm getting into Miss Noonan's bright red car. They must be dying of envy, but I'm way too scared to enjoy this. *Please, please let Granny be all right!*

Miss Noonan is a very fast driver. I'm a bit frazzled when she cuts someone off, but I keep my mouth shut. When we're sitting at a red light that's taking ages, she suddenly says, "So how are things going, Hope? Generally?"

Generally? What does that mean? I freeze.

"Do you feel like you're settling in okay?"

Doesn't she know I have no friends? The first week, a girl called Nicky smiled at me a lot and asked me if I wanted to go to her house after school one day. I said no because if I said yes, I would have to ask her back to my place, and I never know what kind of mood Mom is going to be in. What if it's one of those days when she stays in her nightie and looks like a mess? Anyway, the other girls in the class have pretty well left me alone since then.

"I'm fine," I say stiffly.

"A little bit of advice," Miss Noonan says. "Try not to be so prickly. You have a beautiful smile. Show it to the world a little more."

I look out the window and don't answer her.

The light changes and Miss Noonan spurts across the intersection. A few more blocks and we're there. She parks in front of the hospital and comes inside with me.

Except when I was born, I've never been in a hospital. It's a very busy place. Most of the people milling around are in ordinary clothes, but I spot some nurses and an important-looking man in a long white coat, who just might be a famous heart surgeon.

Miss Noonan takes me over to the elevators. "You go up on your own. Your mom said fourth floor. Go to the nursing station. I'm in a no-parking zone and I don't want to get towed away." She squeezes my arm. "Everything will be okay."

The elevator stops at the second floor and a nurse pushes on a man in a wheelchair. All he's wearing is a short blue thing that looks like a nightie. He winks at me. I blush and pretend not to notice his hairy legs.

When I get off on the fourth floor, I spot Mom right away in a little sitting area with plastic chairs and a table of magazines at the end of a long hallway. Her eyes are rimmed with red, she's wearing one of her oldest dresses and a brown cardigan, and her hair isn't brushed. "You're here," she says, standing up.

I take a big breath. "It's cancer, isn't it?"

She stares at me. "What?"

"Cancer. I just know it."

"You don't get cancer in one day, Hope, and end up in the hospital. She's had a stroke."

"What's a stroke?"

"It's some kind of brain thing." Mom doesn't sound exactly sure. Tears slide down her cheeks, which scares me to death.

"Is it bad?"

"Not too bad," she whispers. "The doctor said it was a small stroke. They've done a bunch of tests and now she's resting."

I start to cry too, and we wrap our arms around each other and have a great big hug.

"Now," Mom sniffs, "we've got to be brave for Granny."

There are four beds in Granny's room. Two are empty,

the blankets and sheets neatly folded. In the third bed there's a very old woman with a halo of gray hair. Her hands are fluttering and she's mumbling, "Nurse, nurse."

There's a curtain around Granny's bed. Mom pulls it back. Granny is lying under a brown blanket and she's asleep. Quite honestly, she looks the same as ever. Her mouth is open and she's snoring. I admit that a teeny tiny bit of me is disappointed. I didn't want to see anything really scary, like tubes going in and out of her (like I saw on TV once), but she doesn't even look sick.

"There's really no point staying," the nurse whispers behind us. "She'll sleep until morning. And you must be exhausted. You've been here all day."

"I suppose you're right," Mom says. She leans over the bed and kisses Granny. "Bye, Mother. I love you."

I kiss Granny too. The smoke smell is gone and she smells quite nice. Even her orange hair doesn't look all that bad today.

"Nurse, nurse," calls the old woman in the other bed, loudly this time.

The nurse rolls her eyes, which shocks me. I thought all nurses were supposed to be like Florence Nightingale. "I'll be there in a minute, Mrs. Markham," she says.

On the way out, I notice that Mrs. Markham has a lot of flowers, arranged in vases on a shelf and on the little table beside her bed. A woman in a suit is just coming in, carrying more flowers and chirping, "Hi, Auntie!"

In the elevator, Mom leans against the wall and says, "Let's not go home right away. Let's go to a restaurant for supper."

Did I hear right? We never eat in restaurants, except on very special occasions. It costs way too much.

"You pick where," she says.

I think about Jake's Steakhouse and The Pancake Palace. My mouth waters.

Then I think about Mrs. Markham's flowers.

"If we didn't go to a restaurant, could we use the money to buy Granny some flowers?" I ask slowly.

Mom's eyes fill with tears and her voice comes out kind of hoarse. "Of course we could." And she adds, "Oh, Hope, you're so much better than I am. I don't deserve someone as special as you."

There it is again: Mom's dark secret.

· · · · ·

Jingle sleeps with me, not close enough to touch but draped over my feet. He wouldn't eat his dinner and he stalked around the apartment, yowling at nothing for hours. Mom says this may be the first night in his memory that he has spent without Granny. She says that cats sense things.

"It's okay, Jingle," I whisper, reaching down to pat his thick fur. He hisses and scratches my hand. I go to sleep thinking about Granny.

• • • • •

Mom comes into the living room really early in the morning, when it's still dark, and sits on the edge of the pull-out couch.

"I'm awake," I say. "I heard the phone ring."

"It was the hospital," she tells me. "Granny had another stroke. A big one this time. She's gone, Hope."

It takes me a second to understand what Mom means.

Then I burst into tears.

Dear Grace,

Do you believe in heaven? I don't know if I do or don't. I've never even been inside a church and I don't have a clue about that kind of stuff. Right now I really, really want to believe.

I'm so scared because I just can't imagine living without Granny. Sometimes she did embarrassing stuff, and I'd roll my eyes and she'd get mad. Now I just wish I could take all that back. Granny has been in this apartment forever, and she was always the same. She was never sick, or lying down, or not happy to see me. I'm so worried that somehow this is our fault. Would Granny have died if we hadn't moved in here and made her life so crowded with our problems?

It makes me feel sick how much I miss her. Why did she have to die?

Your best friend,
Hope

•••••

Dear Grace,
Mom could only think of three people to invite

to Granny's funeral service: Mrs. Pingham, Mrs. Tomlinson, and Mrs. Ladner. They are Granny's only friends, and they always got together once a week to play bridge.

Maybe not having a lot of friends runs in our family. Look at me. And then there's Mom who has *boy*friends but no real friends.

A fourth person showed up, a man in a black suit. He stood quietly at the back and I kept peeking at him. He was bald except for a fringe, but he had a dashing black mustache. I made up a story that he was a long-lost relative of Granny's, but Mom said that his name was Mr. Pinn and he was Granny's lawyer. He gave Mom a card and told her to call him. He's quite good-looking up close, with very twinkly blue eyes, but unfortunately he's too short for Mom.

Granny was cremated, which means BURNED. Mom says it's what Granny wanted, and I hope she's right. It's awfully final.

The service was at a funeral parlor. I hated the man who was in charge. He talked in a yucky voice, and he mixed up Granny's name and called her Lillian *Janice* King instead of Janet. Granny would have been wild.

Afterward no one knew what to do, so we all (except Mr. Pinn) went to The Pancake Palace, where I had peanut butter-and-banana waffles and a chocolate milkshake.

I threw up everything when I got home.

Granny's ashes are in a box. Mom says that one day we are going to go to New York City and scatter them from the Empire State Building. I absolutely cannot picture this, but she says Granny's dream was to go to New York City and see a play on Broadway, but she never made it. For now, I make Mom keep the ashes in her bedroom where I can't see them. But I can't stop thinking about them.

It seems like all Mom and I do is cry.

Your best friend,
Hope

. . . . .

Dear Grace,
Jingle died yesterday. He stopped eating four days ago and already you could feel his bones under his thick fur. Mom took him to the vet and the

vet said he was really, really old and his kidneys were failing. He put Jingle to sleep. Failed kidneys might be the official reason, but Mom and I think he stopped eating because he couldn't bear to live without Granny. I know how he felt.

Your best friend,
Hope

• • • • •

Dear Grace,
There's only one week left of school. Mom phoned Mr. Hubert and told him I'm too upset to go. The class made cards and Miss Noonan dropped them off at our apartment. I don't feel like looking at them, but Mom says to save them because one day I will want them.

Mr. Hubert said that next year I have to do something called remedial math, but because my reading, writing, and verbal skills are so strong, I get to pass into grade six. Whew!!!

Your best friend,
Hope

P.S. I don't have to see nasty Barbara until September!

$\bullet\bullet\bullet\bullet\bullet$

Dear Grace,

Mom and I got in a horrible argument about Granny's bedroom. Her bed, to be exact. I refuse to sleep in it. I know I'll have nightmares.

"It's silly to keep sleeping in the living room," Mom said.

"Then why don't *you* sleep in Granny's bed and I'll have your bedroom?"

She gave me a long, hard look. "Sometimes, Hope, you say the craziest things."

Me? Crazy? If Granny were here, she'd say, "That's the pot calling the kettle black."

Your best friend,
Hope

Chapter Nine

Yesterday, Mom found the card that the lawyer, Mr. Pinn, gave her in the bottom of her purse. She phoned him and made an appointment to see him this afternoon.

"Can I go too?" I asked her.

"No," she said.

"What do you think he wants?"

Mom shrugged, but her cheeks were pink and she seemed excited so I guess she was hopeful.

Please let it be good news.

So now I'm waiting for Mom to come back. I hear her key in the door (I have strict orders to keep it locked when I'm home alone), and I jump up from my book to let her in.

"Well?" I demand.

"Put the kettle on," Mom says, "and make some tea and I'll tell you all about it."

This is totally maddening, but the tea is finally ready and we sit down across from each other at the kitchen table.

"Okay," she says.

"Okay *what*?"

"Granny left a will. She had a tiny bit of savings. Enough to pay the rent for a few more months."

"We won't have to move right away," I say.

"That's right." Mom takes a sip of tea and I see that her hand is shaking. "But there's more, Hope. Mr. Pinn says the last time he saw Granny, about ten years ago, she told him she had purchased a life insurance policy."

"What does that mean?"

"It means that when she dies, a sum of money goes to her beneficiary. I'm pretty sure the beneficiary would be me."

I digest this astounding news. "How much money?"

"He doesn't know. He doesn't even know for sure if she took the policy out. He has no paperwork for it. He suggested we look through Granny's things to see if we can find something." She blinks back sudden tears.

I gulp down the last of my tea. "What *exactly* are we searching for?"

"Official-looking papers." Mom wipes her eyes. "They

might say *Sun Life* at the top. Mr. Pinn says lots of people take out life insurance policies with that company."

It's like a treasure hunt.

I leap up. "We can start now!"

• • • • •

Mom goes right to the big old roll-top desk in the living room. It's our best bet. I tackle Granny's dresser in her bedroom. There are five drawers, all of them sticky and hard to pull out.

The first drawer is full of panties, slips, and stockings. It's embarrassing to paw through them. I would be mortified if someone touched my underwear, and I can imagine Granny peering over my shoulder with her lips pursed. It also makes me feel a little sad because the truth is, Granny's underwear is very plain. I've seen Mom dressing up to go out on one of her dates and she has gorgeous things: black slips, bras with lace, and silky stockings.

Flannel nighties fill the second drawer.

The next two drawers are stuffed with cardigans – all the same but different colors. I pull all of them out. They smell of cigarette smoke. The wool has gone pilly, and one cardigan is missing three buttons.

The fifth drawer is empty except for a plastic bag

containing the pieces of the Royal Doulton figurine I smashed. Cripes.

No official papers of any kind.

Mom appears in the doorway. "Don't put Granny's clothes back in the drawers," she says. "We'll donate them to the thrift shop."

I know Granny's dead, and I know she's never coming back, but I feel sick when Mom says that.

I don't tell Mom that the thrift shop won't want most of this stuff. She's been crying again. Tears have left a smudgy trail through the powder on her cheeks. She watches me while I stack the cardigans in a neat pile.

"Did you find anything in the desk?" I ask.

She shakes her head. "Just a lot of old bank statements and stubs from bills. Envelopes. And elastic bands. Granny had eight unopened packages of elastic bands. Now, why would she want all those elastic bands?"

Her voice goes funny and her shoulders collapse. "I can't face this right now," she says. "I need to go out."

My heart sinks. I know exactly where she means, and I don't want to go.

Chapter Ten

We walk along our street, past two more apartment buildings and some tall, narrow houses, to the park at the end of the block. It's not a real park, just a big square of grass, one city block long on each side. There are some trees in the middle, a play area with swings, a teeter-totter, and a roundabout.

It's not a great day to go to a park. It's damp and chilly, and even though it's June, it doesn't feel like summer. The park is empty except for two girls in puffy jackets. I've never seen them before. They look about my age and they're sitting on the ends of the teeter-totter. One girl is perched in the air and the other has her feet resting on the ground. They're not going up and down, they're just talking, and the girl in the air is swinging her legs back and forth.

Mom and I sit on a bench. I'm wearing a T-shirt and pedal pushers and I'm freezing. Beside me, Mom twists her hands together. She's only wearing a sleeveless dress and one of Granny's thin cardigans, but Mom never feels cold.

The girl in the air glances over at us. She has short black hair and a thin, pointy face. She leans forward and whispers something to the other girl, who has long blonde hair, almost to her waist.

I feel my cheeks turn red. I'm positive she said something about us. "Let's go home," I say.

"We just got here," Mom says.

She has this weird thing about parks. She likes to go and just sit in them. And she drags me along. I've probably been to Stanley Park more than a hundred times. We go to lots of smaller parks too, scattered all over Vancouver.

Mom especially likes parks with playgrounds. I swear she knows where every playground in Vancouver is. When I was little, I loved it. She has a big map of Vancouver, and she would spread it out on the table and pick a park to go to. We would pack a snack of cookies and juice and walk or take the bus. We went every Saturday. I would play on the swings and the jungle gym and scream, "Look at me! Look at me!"

"I see you," she'd say.

When I got a little bit older, though, I realized that Mom wasn't just watching me. She was watching all the kids who came to the playground.

I don't play on the equipment anymore. I usually take a book along, but Mom still stares at the other kids.

It's creepy. It's like she's looking for someone, but I haven't the foggiest idea who. Why does she *do* this?

Now she's watching the girls on the teeter-totter. I pray that they don't notice, but they do. The girl with the pointy face calls out, "Only monkeys stare!"

I am suddenly spitting mad at Mom. I stand up.

"Where are you going?"

"Home. I'm not going to spy on people with you anymore. It's sick."

I march off. When I look back, the girls have moved farther away from Mom, to the swings, and they lean their heads close together and burst out laughing. Mom is still sitting on the bench and she's still staring.

Doesn't she get how crazy she looks?

Dear Grace,

These are the things I want if Mom gets any life insurance:

1. The entire series of *Famous Five* books by Enid Blyton

2. A transistor radio

3. Roller skates

4. A bicycle

5. A trip to Disneyland. Miss Noonan told us about Disneyland. They're building it right now and it won't be open until July 1955. More than a year! But I don't mind waiting. It's going to be the coolest place on earth!!!

Your best friend,
Hope

P.S Three more days 'til my birthday.

Chapter Eleven

Mom and I spend two more days searching for the life insurance policy. The first day we look in all the obvious places. The next day, we look in some not so obvious places, like under the towels in the cupboard in the bathroom, and behind the boxes of cereal in the kitchen.

We forget about eating dinner until almost nine o'clock, and then I make peanut butter sandwiches for both of us. Mom eats the middle, but leaves the crusts. She kisses me good night and disappears into her bedroom. I pull out the living-room couch into a bed, get settled, and open my book, but I fall asleep before I get to the bottom of the page. The next thing I know, I look at my watch and it's past midnight, and I have to go to the bathroom desperately.

The door to Granny's bedroom is partly open and the light is on. On my way back from the bathroom, I peek inside. Mom is sitting on the edge of Granny's bed. She's holding a big brown envelope. The floor is covered with heaps of clothes, shoes, hatboxes, and bags.

"Mom? What are you doing? It's the middle of the night."

Her eyes are wide, staring. "Oh – you scared me. I decided to take everything out of Granny's closet. In case we missed something."

I look at the brown envelope. "You found it!"

She looks me straight in the eye without blinking. "No, I didn't. There are just some of Granny's old letters in here. Nothing important." But she's shaking. There are beads of sweat above her lip and she's as white as a ghost. Something is wrong and I feel scared.

"Are you sick?"

"Of course not. Go back to bed, Hope. Please."

"But –"

She closes her eyes. "Please," she whispers.

I go to bed, but I can't get to sleep.

That thing where Mom looked me straight in the eye without blinking? I do that too – when I tell a lie.

So Mom was lying.

What did she find in that envelope that she doesn't want me to see?

I wiggle around on the couch, trying to find a spot where the metal bits don't jab me. I toss and turn. I can't shut my brain off. I roll over on my stomach, and these are some of the crazy thoughts leaping around in my head like jumping beans:

Will nasty Barbara Porter be in my class next year?

Is it against the law to throw Granny's ashes off the Empire State Building?

Can you be a war hero if you die of food poisoning?

I flip onto my back and kick at the sheet twisted around my ankles.

Will Mom remember that it's my birthday tomorrow?

What's in that big brown envelope?

Chapter Twelve

I sleep in, and for once Mom is up before me. She's in the kitchen making blueberry pancakes, which I didn't even know she knew how to make. On the table there are four small identical oblong presents wrapped in old wrinkled Christmas paper. Not big enough to be roller skates or a radio. Anyway, I know what they are. I can tell by the shape. Books.

"Happy birthday, eleven-year-old," Mom says.

I burst into noisy sobs. She drops her spoon and sweeps me into her arms. "What ever is the matter?"

"I don't know," I blubber into her nightie.

How can I tell her that she scared me last night? And that I thought we were going to be rich and now we're not?

And that for once I hoped I might get a surprise for my birthday? It makes me look like a horrible person.

I sniff and wipe my eyes and say, "Can I open my presents before I eat?"

"Why not?"

Four Nancy Drew books – *The Secret of the Wooden Lady*, *The Clue of the Black Keys*, *The Mystery at the Ski Jump*, and *The Clue of the Velvet Mask* – and they're brand-new!

"Perfect, Mom." I really mean it.

I prop the books up around me while I eat my pancakes. "Can we go out for dinner?"

She doesn't say anything.

Cripes. Now I feel guilty because she's spent a lot of money on all these books.

"I thought I'd cook us a steak for a treat," she says finally. "I picked one up yesterday."

"Great," I say, but I don't think I fooled her.

"But I don't think I can cope with a cake." She pushes her hair off her face. She looks wiped and there's a smear of blueberry on her nose. "I'm not really a baker and store-bought ones cost…"

Mom's voice trails off. It was always Granny who made my cake. Every year was different. My favorite one had a little swimming pool, made out of a tin-foil bowl and blue Jell-O, right in the middle of the cake! I don't want a cake anyway, not without Granny to watch me blow out my candles.

I rinse my syrupy plate under the tap, but Mom says, "Get away from here. No dishes for the birthday girl."

She reaches for her purse and gives me twenty-five cents for public swimming at the community center.

I'd like enough money for a pop and fries after my swim, but I don't ask.

• • • • •

Mom and I leave the apartment together after lunch. She has an interview at the Hudson's Bay store downtown to be an elevator operator.

I try to keep my mouth shut, but I can't help it. "Don't you think you should dress up a bit more?"

She's wearing an old gray skirt and a white blouse, and she's put on her cherry lipstick but no other makeup. An elevator operator should look glamorous. I remember when she went for the store clerk interview and Granny said she looked like a million dollars.

Mom sighs. "Oh, what's the use? I'm not going to get the job anyway."

As we wait at the bus stop, I say in this goofy sing-song voice, "Fourth floor, ladies lingerie…fifth floor, men's shoes." All I get out of her is a tiny smile.

Mom catches the bus right before mine. I climb onto number 12, which will take me to the community center in the neighborhood where we were living last summer. There's probably a pool closer to our apartment, but I'm used to this one. Granny paid for me to take swimming lessons and I practically lived there the whole month of August, zipping through the Red Cross levels.

Granny said that I'm a fish and that I came by it honestly. When Mom was a teenager, she swam all the way across Cultus Lake and raised a hundred dollars. She gave every penny of it to the Salvation Army. Granny said no one could beat Mom in swimming. I've never been to Cultus Lake and Mom doesn't ever swim anymore, but we have a newspaper article all about it, so I know it's true.

The pool is outside, surrounded by a chain-link fence. The lifeguard is my swimming teacher from last summer. His name is Joe and he looks like a lifeguard should – shaggy blond hair and a tan, even though we've only had a few sunny days all month.

He remembers me. "Hi, Hope," he says. "How come you aren't in school?"

"It's my birthday." I don't want to explain anymore. I especially don't want to talk about Granny. He gives me a thumbs-up.

The pool is empty. I swim laps up and down, up and down.

Joe climbs down off his lifeguard chair and teaches me how to do a tuck turn at the end of each lap. I'm grinning underwater. I love the power of pushing off the wall with my feet and surging forward like a seal. Joe yells, "Way to go, kid!" each time I come to the surface.

When I'm totally exhausted, I float on my back and think about the big brown envelope. What was in it? Why did Mom look so upset?

The sky is full of dark gray clouds and a few raindrops plop into my eyes. My feet bump into the ladder and I pull myself onto the bottom rung. The clock on the wall reads three-thirty. School's over.

Kids start pouring in, and Joe scrambles back up on his chair. I spot two of the popular girls from my old school, dipping their toes in at the steps and screeching that it's cold. They're wearing great bathing suits, one lime green and one bright yellow. I feel stupid in my suit, which is last year's plain navy, and too small. I climb up the ladder, say good-bye to Joe, and flee to the changing room before the girls can see me.

It's raining cats and dogs when I leave the community center. By the time I get home, I'm soaked. The first thing I see when I unlock the apartment door is Mom's purse on the little hall table. There's a note beside it in her handwriting.

Job was already taken by the time I got there. Just my luck!!! Wake me up no later than 6.

xoxox Mom

I have a hot shower and wash all the chlorine out of my hair. I shampoo and rinse three times because I've heard that too much chlorine can turn your hair green. Then I curl up in Granny's recliner in the living room with *The Clue of the Velvet Mask*.

At six o'clock, I open Mom's bedroom door a crack and peer at her. Her skirt, blouse, and stockings are draped over a chair and she's wearing a pale pink slip. She's lying on her side on her bed, one arm draped across her face, and snoring ever so gently.

I head to the kitchen and inspect the fridge. The steak is sitting on a plate, but I haven't the foggiest idea how to cook it. I pour myself a bowl of cornflakes and take it into the living room.

I pull out the couch and make it into my bed. Then I prop myself up with my cornflakes and I read right to the very last page of my book. It's midnight when I turn out the light. I can't stop yawning. As Granny would say, I'm so tired I could sleep on a clothesline.

My first day of being eleven is over.

Chapter Thirteen

I go to the pool every day for the rest of the week. Joe gives me free pointers and I can feel my strokes getting stronger.

On Friday, he says to me, "I'm starting a swim team this summer. How about joining? You're good enough."

Swim teams must cost money and Mom has already told me she can't afford lessons this year. The twenty-five cents a day is all she can manage and I don't even know how long that's going to last. But it's way too embarrassing to tell Joe that. So I just shrug and say, "I'll think about it."

On the way out, I squeeze through a bunch of kids who are lined up to pay to come in. They're noisier than usual and the boys are pushing and shoving each other. I suddenly remember that today is the last day of school and it's now summer holidays. Cripes! Now I won't have the pool and Joe to myself anymore.

I get off the bus a few blocks before my stop because I feel like walking. The sun is finally out. It's warm and the air smells like flowers and mown grass. I love summer.

Then I get opposite the park and spot Mom.

She's perched on her usual bench, staring at a bunch of girls who are sitting cross-legged in a circle on the grass. They're all girls from my school.

That nasty Barbara Porter is right in the middle, waving her arms around as she tells a story.

Any minute, they're going to look up and see this crazy woman watching them.

What if they figure out she's my mother?

I break into a run. I don't breathe normally again until I am safely inside our apartment.

I dump my wet towel and bathing suit in the bathroom sink. I rinse my hair in the shower and then go into the living room and plunk down in Granny's recliner.

I tilt Granny's chair back and remember how I had to beg for turns to sit in it. Granny hated the way I would make the chair crash back and forth, like a ship in the sea.

I gaze around the room. It looks exactly like it did when Granny was alive: cluttered with ornaments and lace doilies and spindly tables. When I was little and we visited

Granny, Mom was always afraid I would break something. Every Sunday, Granny lifted down all her Royal Doulton china figurines from the tall cabinet in the corner of the living room. She set them on the dining room table and dusted each one with a soft cloth. When I turned seven, she said I was old enough to help.

As we dusted, Granny told me the story of when she got each one. I fell in love with them. The Balloon Man with his bundle of colorful balloons, The Shepherd with a tiny lamb, Suzette holding up her flowered pink dress. Granny saved up from her pension checks and bought a new one each year.

They haven't been dusted for weeks. Granny would feel terrible. I find the dusting cloth and then I take the figurines out of the cabinet and put them on the dining room table, one at a time. I have to get a chair to stand on to reach Shy Anne and The Lady of the Fan, who are on the top shelf.

The chair is wobbly and I'm teetering a bit and I can feel Granny's sharp eyes on me.

That's when I spot it.

A long, white envelope, leaning against the back of the cabinet behind Shy Anne.

I slide it out with my fingers.

On the front, in Granny's handwriting, are the words *Sun Life Insurance Policy.*

Dear Grace,

I found the life insurance policy!!!!

Five thousand dollars!!!!

We're RICH RICH RICH!!!!

Mom was at the park but as soon as she got home she phoned Granny's lawyer, Mr. Pinn. He was just leaving work for the weekend, but he said he'd call her on Saturday since it was so important.

Then we got all dressed up and went to Jake's Steakhouse to celebrate.

"Five thousand dollars," Mom sighed. "That'll keep the wolves from the door."

That's what Granny used to say every time her old age pension check came in the mail.

For a few minutes, a cloud slid over everything. I could tell Mom was remembering too.

It's just too darn awful that getting the life insurance means that Granny had to die. But Mom says that Granny would want us to be happy.

Your best friend,
Hope

• • • • •

Dear Grace,

Mr. Pinn took Mom to a fancy restaurant for lunch today. She wore her sunflower dress. He told her it will probably take a month to get the money. He's going to contact Sun Life Insurance right away. He told Mom she should invest most of it (investing means that the money will grow even more!!), but Mom says we will spend some of it on treats.

I get to join the swim team!

Your best friend,
Hope

P.S. Guess what happened this afternoon. The doorbell rang and it was a boy from the florist shop with an enormous bouquet of pink flowers!! Mom says they're carnations and that Mr. Pinn sent them because he feels bad about Granny. No one has EVER sent us flowers before!

P.P.S. I wonder if eleven is too old to keep writing to an imaginary friend.

Oh heck! Who cares?

Chapter Fourteen

I've opened all the windows in the apartment and a fresh breeze is blowing in. Is it disloyal to want to blow all the stale cigarette smell out of the curtains and rugs? It's not like I'm trying to get rid of Granny. She's been gone for exactly forty-two days now and that's a fact, and even though I still miss her tons, it doesn't hurt quite as bad.

I'm by myself because Mom has gone to Queen Elizabeth Park. I refused to go (it's about time I took a stand). Music from the ice-cream man's truck drifts up from the street. I dig six cents out of the jug in the kitchen and run out of the apartment and down the two flights of stairs. The ice-cream man knows me and hands me a lime Popsicle without me saying a word.

I've had a lime Popsicle every day for three weeks now. I don't think I will ever get sick of lime Popsicles! I sit in the sun on the steps outside the apartment building and lick it slowly.

Summer is going by way too fast. One more week and July will be over. I get this knot in my stomach when I think about school starting again, so I think about the swim team instead. We practice every morning from six-thirty until nine o'clock. At first it was torture to get up so early, but now I kind of like it. I'm the only passenger on the bus at six o'clock and the driver and I have gotten quite friendly. When he sees me, he always says, "The early bird catches the worm," which makes me think of Granny.

Green lime juice is running down my arm. My Popsicle is collapsing and I finish it off in a couple of bites. I watch the postman. He's swinging along the sidewalk toward me, whistling.

I wait outside while he fills the silver boxes in the downstairs hall in our building.

"See you, squirt," he says, bounding past me down the steps.

Our old box belongs to someone else now and our mail is forwarded to Granny's box. We hardly ever get anything, but I go upstairs and get the key and then come back down to check.

Today there *is* something – a big square white envelope. It feels stiff, like there might be cardboard inside. It's addressed to Granny and there's no return address. I take it up to our apartment and put it on the kitchen table and stare at it. Up until now, when mail comes for Granny, Mom opens it. But I'm curious.

I tear back the flap at the top of the envelope and slide out a photograph. It's of a girl, about my age. It's not the kind of picture you take quickly. Instead, it looks like she was posing for it. The girl is sitting on a chair and there's a blue background, like a fake sky with painted clouds, behind her. She's all dressed up in a navy dress with a white collar and white buttons down the front and she has curly brown hair and blue eyes.

Who is she?

I turn the photograph over.

On the back someone has written in flowing handwriting

Grace
June 23, 1954

Grace!

June 23! My birthday!

I feel like I have been punched in the stomach. I sink into a chair.

Who is she?

I turn the photograph over and study her face again. I have never seen her before in my life. Why did she have her picture taken on my birthday? And who sent it to Granny?

There's nothing on the outside or inside of the envelope to give me a clue.

I look at the back of the photograph again.

Grace.

I notice some more writing in the bottom corner. It's in black ink and looks like it was done with a stamp. It says: *Hal Rhodes Photography Studio, Harrison Hot Springs, BC.*

I've never heard of Harrison Hot Springs.

And there's only one Grace that I know. She's mine and she's private and I don't understand why her name is on the back of this photograph.

I'm still sitting at the kitchen table when I hear Mom's key in the door. She's carrying a paper bag of groceries; she comes into the kitchen and dumps it on the kitchen counter. "How was swim –"

Her voice breaks off. She stares at me and then at the photograph on the kitchen table. Her face goes dead white.

I swallow.

"Who is Grace?" I manage to ask.

Chapter Fifteen

"I can't talk about this right now," Mom says.

"You *have* to!"

Mom and I stare at each other.

"Who is Grace?" My voice is shaking.

Mom leans against the counter. She suddenly looks old and very tired, and I feel a tiny pang of pity. But I need to know.

"*Mom!*"

She pushes back a strand of her hair. Her eyes swim with tears. "I don't know where to begin," she says.

I harden my heart. I'm fed up with Mom's crying. "You could start with the truth." I pick up the photograph. "Her name is on the back. Grace. So is my birthday. Who is she?"

At first I don't think Mom is going to answer me. She takes a tissue out of the box on the counter and wipes her eyes. She sits down beside me at the table. She reaches out her hand as if she is going to touch the photograph, but then she pulls back.

Outside the kitchen window, a lawn mower rumbles. Some kids shout. It's a normal day. But it's not normal in here. My heart is thumping in my ears.

"Grace is your sister," Mom says finally.

Her voice is so soft and I think I must have heard her wrong.

"*What?*"

"Your sister." Mom twists her hands together in a knot. "You want the truth, Hope, so here it is. Grace is your twin sister."

Is this some kind of joke? Is she serious?

"What are you saying?" I whisper.

Mom bites her lip so hard I think she is going to make it bleed.

"*Mom.* You have to tell me."

"You have a twin sister. Her name is Grace. I gave her up for adoption when you were both two and a half years old."

Mom covers her face with her hands. "This is hard for me to talk about."

"Hard for you? What about me?" My voice is getting

louder and louder, but I don't care. "I don't get it. Grace is real? All this time I thought she was someone I made up; and now you're telling me she's real?"

"Yes."

"And you just gave her away?"

"Yes." Mom looks at me now. "No, not like that. I didn't just give her away. I couldn't look after her."

"Why not? You looked after me. Why couldn't you look after her?"

Mom is silent.

"Well, why couldn't you look after her?"

"She had polio," Mom says.

Polio.

The word sends a shiver through me. I've only known one kid with polio. Her name was Patty and she was in my grade two class. She had metal braces on both her legs. I remember feeling so sorry for her.

"It was hard enough having twins." Tears slide down Mom's cheeks. "I was only nineteen when you were born. I was exhausted all the time. And then Grace got polio. She was in this iron lung in the hospital and the doctor said that when she finally came home she would need all kinds of special care – hot compresses every two hours and exercises. I couldn't do it. I just couldn't do it."

"So you gave her away."

"There was a nurse at the hospital. Her name was Sharon Donnely. She fell in love with Grace. She worked in the polio ward. She knew how to do all the things for Grace. And she and her husband, Bill, couldn't have children of their own, and they desperately wanted a child. We talked, and then…"

Mom's voice trails off.

I can't believe what I'm hearing. "What about me? Didn't I wonder where Grace had gone?"

"You did at first. But you were little and I think after awhile you forgot you had a sister."

"Because you lied to me. You told me Grace was imaginary. That I had made her up. You and Granny. You both *lied* to me."

Mom puts her hand on mine, but I jerk away.

I'm crying now too. "How can she be my twin?" I gulp through my sobs. "She doesn't look at all like me."

A sudden thought hits me. I stare at the photograph again. Curly brown hair. Blue eyes. A perfect nose. "She looks like you."

"You're fraternal twins," Mom says, "not identical twins. You were totally different, right from the day you were born."

She hesitates. "There are more pictures. Granny hid them in her cupboard. I didn't know. I found them when

76

we were looking for the life insurance. Sharon and I had agreed that we wouldn't have any contact, but Granny must have talked to her. Granny was so upset when Grace went. She must have made Sharon agree to send a picture every year on your birthday."

The big brown envelope. I feel sick. I hate Mom – I really hate her.

I stand up. "I don't want to see any more pictures. And I don't want to talk about this anymore."

"I'm sorry," she whispers. "I'm so sorry."

I swipe at my wet cheeks. "No you're not."

I take a big shuddery breath. "If I had gotten sick would you have given me away too?"

Mom looks like I have slapped her.

"How can you call yourself a mother?" I shout.

I run out of the kitchen.

• • • • •

I think I've only been asleep for a hundred seconds, but when I turn on the light beside the couch and look at my watch it's two o'clock, the middle of the night. Mom had made me a grilled cheese sandwich for my supper but I refused to eat it. So the last thing I ate was the lime Popsicle, but I don't feel hungry.

I have a sister. It's like a voice keeps saying that over and over in my head, but I still don't believe it.

I get out of bed and peer out the living-room window. It's raining lightly and the street is slick and black in the yellowish light from the street lamp.

Grace isn't my imaginary friend. She's my *sister.* How could Mom have kept that a secret?

When I turn back to bed, I notice a big brown envelope on the table beside the couch. My heart jumps. Mom must have sneaked in while I was sleeping.

I tip the envelope onto my bed and a stack of photographs slides out. The one on top is the one I've already seen. The others are in order and I lay each one on my rumpled sheets. I study Grace's face as she gets younger and younger. She is smiling in all the pictures and she seems to always be changing her hair: short, long, braids, high pigtails. Even in the braids, you can see the curls escaping around her face.

When I get to the last picture, I feel like I've been hit in the stomach. There are braces on Grace's legs. Like Patty in my second grade class.

"*Polio.*"

I whisper the word, but it sounds as loud as a drum in my ears. I turn the photograph over. The same flowing letters.

Grace. June 23, 1947

1947 was seven years ago. She was four. I don't know what she looked like before that. I don't know what she looked like the last time I saw her. I close my eyes. I try to force my brain to remember, but I can't.

A lump presses in my throat. I *can't* remember.

What would it be like to have braces on your legs? Heavy. Clumsy. Ugly. I remember Patty crying once at recess because her legs hurt.

Grace looks normal in the other photographs, but she's sitting down and you can't really tell if there is anything wrong with her legs. I look on the backs of all the photographs. Starting from 1949, they all have the same stamp in the bottom corner.

Hal Rhodes Photography Studio, Harrison Hot Springs, BC.

Tears sting my eyes and my nose starts to run.

I have a sister. And I can't even remember one tiny thing about her. This is the worst thing that has ever happened to me.

Suddenly I want Mom.

She's not in her bedroom or in the kitchen. The apartment is so quiet it's eerie. I can hear the fridge humming.

Just like that, I know where Mom is. My hands

fumbling, I take off my pajamas and put on a pair of shorts and a T-shirt. I throw on a jacket and dash out of the apartment. I should be scared stiff to be outside in the middle of the night, but I'm not. I race down the street, the rain like mist on my face. I run all the way to the park.

Mom is sitting on her bench. She's in her nightie and her hair is in wet, stringy ringlets around her shoulders. I can't tell if it's rain or tears on her face.

I sit down beside her.

She's shivering so hard it frightens me.

It's weird. I was so mad at Mom, but my anger has disappeared. And even though right now she looks crazier than ever, I know that my mom is not crazy. All these years, she's been missing Grace.

I hold Mom's hand. It feels like ice.

"I saw her at Stanley Park once," Mom says. "You and Granny had gone to get an ice-cream cone and I saw her coming out of the washroom with Sharon. She was little. Four years old. I saw the braces first and I thought, *That little girl has polio*, and then I saw that it was Grace."

"Did she see you?" I say.

"No. I turned around until they were gone. But I went to their house a few months later. I knew where they lived. I was going to tell Sharon I couldn't do it like this anymore. I needed to see Grace."

Mom is quiet then. Shivering even harder.

"What happened?" I ask.

"There were different people living there," Mom whispers. "They told me an awful thing. Sharon and Bill had been killed in a car accident. It must have happened soon after I saw Grace."

"Killed?" My stomach flips over. "What did you do?"

"I couldn't do anything. They said they had heard that a great-aunt had taken Grace. But they didn't know the aunt's name or where she lived." Mom's voice wobbles. "A great-aunt. She might be really old. I don't want someone really old raising Grace."

"Granny was sort of old," I say. I don't add that a lot of the time Granny looked after me more than Mom did.

Mom pulls her hand away from mine. She twists her fingers together. "Losing her parents like that. I can't bear to think of Grace going through that."

Her parents. For a second, I don't know who she means. Then I realize that she's talking about the people who adopted Grace, the people called Sharon and Bill.

People that Mom hardly knew. I push that thought away. I don't want to blame Mom for any of this. She sounds so sad, and I don't know what to do.

"I really thought I would find Grace again one day," Mom says. "I thought that maybe she liked parks and I would find her in a park. Stupid idea, right?"

"Not really," I say.

"I don't know if she's okay, Hope. I don't know if she's happy."

"I don't think the great-aunt lives in Vancouver," I say slowly. "I think she lives in a place called Harrison Hot Springs. It's on the back of the photographs."

Mom stares at me. Her blue eyes look dark, like the ocean on a cloudy day.

"We could go there, Mom. To Harrison Hot Springs. Wherever that is."

I take a big breath. It's the only thing that will make Mom better.

"We could find Grace."

Part Two

HARRISON HOT SPRINGS, 1954

Chapter Sixteen

We don't leave for a week. There are so many things to do. Mom talks to Mr. Pinn about the life insurance money. He promises to make some phone calls and two days later Mom comes home with three crisp one hundred dollar bills.

"The rest is in the bank," she says.

I've never seen a one hundred dollar bill before. And we have three of them!

I go down to the pool and tell Joe I'll be away for a while.

Mom checks the bus schedule. A Pacific Coach Lines bus leaves for Harrison Hot Springs every day at eleven o'clock. Mr. Pinn is a gold mine of information about Harrison Hot Springs. He told Mom it's a little village in the Fraser Valley, tucked at the end of Harrison Lake, which is huge. He says people go to the famous Harrison Hot Springs Hotel to swim in the pools, which are heated by the hot springs. The bus trip is a milk run. That means it stops in all the little towns on the way. It will take us more than three hours to get there.

I pack my suitcase. I stuff in shorts, T-shirts, underwear, my bathing suit, *The Secret of the Wooden Lady* and *The Clue of the Black Keys* (which I plan to read over again), my hippo, Harry, and my Dear Grace letters. I figure the letters might give me luck. I don't know if it's going to be hard or easy to find Grace.

Mom almost changes her mind. "I don't think I can do this."

"You can."

"We probably won't find her."

"We will. Mr. Pinn said there are only about three hundred people living in Harrison Hot Springs. How hard can it be to find one person in three hundred?"

That makes Mom smile.

I wish I felt as sure as I sound. The plan seemed perfect when I thought of it. Find Grace and Mom will stop being so sad. But what if it doesn't work that way? What if it makes Mom worse?

And there is another question chewing away at me. If we find Grace, what are we going to do then?

• • • • •

The Pacific Coach Lines bus is better than the city bus. It's bigger and the seats are comfortable with high backs. The driver stows our suitcases underneath the bus, and I scramble up the steps to grab a seat near the middle of the bus by the window. Mom sits across the aisle from me. There are only a few other people who get on, and they go to the back.

It takes a long time to get out of Vancouver. The bus makes a couple of stops and more people get on. Just when I think the city is going to go on forever, green fields with black-and-white cows in them, barns, and farmhouses appear. For a while, I keep track of the towns where the bus stops – Maple Grove, Haney, and Mission.

Eventually, I slide across the aisle and sit beside Mom. I dig in the bag by her feet for a bologna-and-mustard sandwich. Mom is asleep, her head pressed up against the window. She looks beat. I've gotten her this far anyway, which is a small miracle.

Three bites into my sandwich and I suddenly feel sick and can't eat any more. If Granny were here, she would say it was nerves. If I have to be honest, a teeny tiny bit of me is scared, but mostly I'm excited.

I have a twin sister!

The thing is, I know something about twins. I read all the Bobbsey Twin books when I was little and I've read other books with twins in them. So I'm pretty sure that when I meet Grace, we will have an instant bond. We'll probably be telepathic and know each other's thoughts.

I told that to Mom last night and she got a funny look on her face and said, "First we have to find her."

• • • • •

The bus is hot and stuffy and I'm starting to doze a little too, when the driver announces the town of Agassiz. I jerk bolt upright in my seat and then lean over to poke Mom awake. Agassiz is the last town before Harrison Hot Springs. A lot of people get off, and then we are on our way again. We pass a few farms, but mostly the view out the window is forest.

The trees are blowing in the wind and raindrops spatter against the window. The road is twisty and the bus sways on the corners.

Suddenly houses spring up on both sides of the road. I spot a sign that says *Camping*, a gas station, a café, and a bright blue shack with a giant wooden ice-cream cone on the sidewalk in front of it. The bus is heading straight toward a huge stretch of choppy gray water, which must be the lake Mr. Pinn talked about. I think we're going to drive right into the lake when the bus swings to the left. A minute later, it rumbles to a stop.

"Last stop!" the driver calls out cheerfully. "Harrison Hot Springs!"

We spill off the bus and all of the passengers mill around for a few minutes, waiting while the driver opens the compartment underneath and unloads suitcases and bags onto the pavement. The bus is parked in front of a huge bubble-gum pink building with a white roof and windows with white frames. A man in a spiffy gray uniform is standing under a pink-and-white striped awning. A fancy sign says *Harrison Hot Springs Hotel.* I feel like I'm in a fairy tale.

A cold wind is blowing; I hop up and down while I wait impatiently for Mom, who is the last one off the bus. By then the other passengers have disappeared. The bus rumbles away and we're left standing there beside our suitcases.

The wind wraps Mom's turquoise skirt tight around her long legs, her hair is wild and flying everywhere. It's obvious that the man in the uniform can't take his eyes off her. "Are you coming into the hotel?" he calls out. "Can I help you with your luggage?"

Mom hesitates. "I think so. Maybe." She sighs. "I mean, yes, thank you."

He's very helpful, jumping to grab our suitcases, opening the glass door, and ushering us inside. No one has ever held a door open for me before. I feel like Queen Elizabeth. I look around in awe. We're in a pale blue room with bright red furniture. There's a totem pole in the corner and four super-tall trees with skinny white trunks. (Real trees *inside* the hotel! I'm not kidding!)

"Outlandish," Mom murmurs beside me. "What on earth is this going to cost?"

"We've got three hundred dollars," I remind her in a whisper.

"But it's got to last." A frown crinkles Mom's forehead. "There are bound to be lots of motor courts in this town. They'll be cheaper. Maybe we should look around."

"I want to stay here. Please, please, *please.*"

Mom sighs. "No promises. Watch our suitcases while I ask."

She goes up to a counter with a sign that says *Reception* and I peer into another room. There's more white trees in there and an enormous fireplace made out of stones. A table is set with teacups and teapots and plates with cookies and pieces of cake. People are perched on sofas and armchairs, holding teacups and napkins and chatting. I wish I had enough nerve to steal a cookie.

Mom is taking a long time. I cross my fingers. I am

eleven years old and I have never stayed in a hotel in my whole entire life.

Then Mom is back. She's holding a shiny gold key. And she's smiling.

Chapter Seventeen

I adore our room. Mom says they told her at the desk that it's called French Provincial, which sounds so *elegant*. It has blue-and-white curtains that go from the ceiling all the way to the floor, a ginormous bed with puffy pillows, and two chairs covered in purple velvet.

We even have our own bathroom with a gigantic bathtub on curved feet, stacks of thick towels, and soaps wrapped in pale pink paper. I try some lotion from a glass container and test the taps, which gush with steaming hot water.

When I come back into the room, Mom is flipping through a skinny yellow phone book. "There's no Donnely in here. There are only a couple of pages for Harrison Hot Springs. And there's no Donnely."

For a second, I don't know what Mom's talking about. Then I remember that Donnely was the last name of Sharon, the nurse who adopted Grace. I guess I just thought that Grace's last name would be King, like mine.

"What does that prove?"

Mom sighs. "Nothing. I suppose the great-aunt could have a different last name. Her name would be listed in here, not Grace's."

Mom kicks off her shoes and lies on the bed. I plunk down at the desk and examine the contents of the drawer. There's a black Bible, cream paper with *Harrison Hot Springs Hotel* written in fancy writing at the top, envelopes, a pen, and a book filled with pages about the hotel.

"There's two pools, one inside and one outside," I report to Mom as I flip through the book. "The indoor pool is sulfur and you can *drink* sulfur water every day if you want – UCK! – and you can have something called a massage salt rub. And there are movies on Friday nights, and they serve tea every afternoon in the lounge. It says it's complimentary."

"That means it's free," Mom says.

I keep reading. "You can borrow bicycles. And, oh, there's a menu here and – *HOLY TOLEDO* – you can get food sent to your room!"

Mom winces. "Don't shout. It's called room service. All good hotels have room service."

"Are you serious? Do you think it's complimentary? Can we order something?"

"No."

Mom doesn't sound too good. Her voice has brittle edges. When she gets like this, I'm sometimes afraid she's going to shatter into a thousand pieces, like a piece of glass, and disappear.

"It's not complimentary," Mom says, "and we're not having it. I made all those sandwiches and I packed you an apple, too. You can take a dollar out of my purse. Now hush and close the curtains. I'm going to stay here for a while."

A dollar! That's four allowances!

There are two gold cords with tassels to pull that make the curtains glide shut. Neat-o. The curtains are made out of really heavy material and the room is dark now. I feel around in Mom's purse for a dollar bill and then slip out the door.

I whisper, "See you later," but if Mom hears me, she doesn't answer.

• • • • •

I'm dying to explore the hotel. I wander up and down the long hallways and get lost twice before I figure out where everything is.

I find the indoor pool first, which is in a big steamy room that smells like boiled eggs. The water is pale green and when I dip my hand in it feels as hot as a bath. There's no one in it except for a man with a big round belly, like a beach ball, who is floating on his back in the shallow end.

I venture down some more hallways and then a sign leads me to The Copper Room. I peer through a doorway into a dining room with tables set with white cloths and glistening silver.

There's a gleaming piano that looks like it's made out of copper. It's as shiny as a mirror. And there's a round polished wooden floor that I bet is for dancing. I get this crazy idea to take my running shoes off and slide around in my socks when a man with a tray of glasses comes through a doorway at the back of the room. I give him a small wave and disappear.

Back in the lounge, the afternoon tea is over. All the guests have left except for a woman reading in the corner and two little girls in bathing suits and bathrobes playing cards at a round table. I manage to grab a leftover piece of yellow cake with gooey icing just as a teenaged girl in a maid's uniform whisks the tray away.

I gulp the cake down in three bites and lick the sticky bits off my fingers. I check out the small gift shop next. It's beside the reception desk and is filled with neat stuff like glass ornaments, perfume, soap, boxes of chocolates and fudge, postcards, books, and even a rack of bathing suits.

"Can I help you find something?" asks a woman with red hair. She has pink glasses, which I admire immensely. If I had glasses, I would get a crazy color too, instead of the boring old glasses that most people have.

I touch the dollar bill in my pocket and then shake my head. I can taste that marshmallow fudge melting in my mouth, but who knows when I'll have a whole dollar again? "No, thank you."

I head outside. Puddles dot the pavement in front of the hotel, but the sun is shining through the clouds and there are patches of blue sky. "Enough blue sky to make a Dutchman a pair of pants," I say, thinking of Granny.

I cross the road and stand in front of a low stone wall that runs along the lake. A couple that I bet anything are newlyweds are taking pictures of each other and giggling a lot. They take breaks to smooch! An older lady with a baby stroller walks past and smiles at me. Two kids race by on bicycles.

The lake is huge and gray, like the ocean. I can see an island and, way in the distance, the peaks of mountains. A motorboat cuts across the water, leaving two frothy lines of wake behind it. It slows down and glides up to the side of a long red dock that juts out into the lake. Three kids wearing bright orange life jackets climb out, shouting at each other and laughing. They look like they're having so much fun.

It's really beautiful. I wish Mom were out here too, looking at everything instead of lying in that dark room feeling sad.

I turn around and gaze back at the hotel. As far as I can tell, the hotel is at the end of the road. If you keep going past it, there's a big hillside covered in forest. A path disappears around a bend. I'll see what's along there later. Right now I want to go in the other direction and see the village.

The road into the village runs right beside the lake. There's the stone wall, a path, and the lake on one side of the road and buildings on the other. There are way more people than I expected out walking around. They look like tourists. You can tell because they're taking their time and they're chatting or licking ice-cream cones or taking pictures. I pass a store called Inkman's, a store called The Red and White, and a couple of cafés. There's an empty lot where some kids are playing baseball, a big white building with flowers at the front, a place with little brown bungalows all exactly the same, and a *No Vacancy* sign. The whole time, I'm looking for Grace, but I don't see her.

In hardly any time at all, I end up at a gravelly beach, which is pretty much the end of the village. At least it is as far as I can go.

Three boys partway down the beach are standing around a pile of boards and arguing in loud voices. I stay away from them and walk across the gravel to the edge of the water. I pick up a smooth round stone and hurl it as far as I can. My stomach feels like it's full of fluttering birds. How am I ever going to find Grace?

I take my running shoes and socks off and wade in the water. I can't get very far past my ankles because it's so icy cold.

The sun has disappeared and the sky has filled up with black clouds. A cold wind is blowing right through my T-shirt. Weather sure changes fast around here. A few raindrops sting my cheeks.

I should be thinking about Grace, but instead I think about the fire in the hotel lounge, the squishy armchairs, and my book. Looking for Grace isn't going to be as simple as I thought. I'm starting to shiver and the thought of going back to the hotel is getting better and better.

I put my socks and shoes back on. I head across the beach and jog down the road.

It's pouring now. The slanted raindrops prick like needles, and all the tourists have disappeared. I slow down beside the Top Notch Café and glimpse through the window at tables crowded with people. My stomach rumbles. It looks so warm and inviting. I'd love an orange float, but I don't want to go in there by myself.

I keep jogging, my head ducked against the rain. I stop outside the store with the sign that says *Inkman's*. I peer through the window. It looks like the kind of store that would sell candy. I have a sudden craving for a stick of black licorice. Or a giant jawbreaker. After all, I have a whole dollar!

I push the door open and a bell jingles.

I take three steps in and then slam to a stop.

There's a counter right across from the door. A girl is standing there with her back to me. She has brown curly hair, her legs are skinny sticks like mine, and we are the same height. Exactly.

The storekeeper is wrapping something in brown paper for her. "Tell your aunt I hope she feels better soon," he says.

I clamp my lips together to stop myself from yelping out loud. My legs turn to jelly.

I've found Grace.

Chapter Eighteen

I can't keep standing in the doorway like a ninny. I have to go in or go out.

I take a deep breath and step inside. I scuttle over to a shelf stacked with boxes of cereal and pretend to be looking at them. I feel like a spy in a secret agent movie. My heart is pounding so loudly that it's a miracle the girl and the storekeeper can't hear it.

"I'll have three jawbreakers," the girl says.

Ohmigosh. She's thinking about jawbreakers too. This is exactly what I mean about the bond between twins.

My legs wobble. The storekeeper glances at me and I give him a confident smile and pick up a box of Shredded Wheat.

Cripes. What do I do now?

A plan. I need a plan. I've spent a lot of time imagining finding Grace, but I've never imagined what to do next.

Then the girl says, "See you later." She turns around.

Her face is covered with freckles.

And when she walks past me, I can see that we aren't the same height at all. She's shorter than me. She looks about eight years old.

The bell jingles and she's gone.

The storekeeper is staring hard at me now. He has bushy gray eyebrows that meet in the middle. "Fifteen cents," he says.

I blink and try to focus. "What?"

"Cereal. Fifteen cents."

He probably thinks I don't have any money. He probably thinks I'm one of those kids that hang around in stores and swipe stuff.

To prove him wrong, I pay for the cereal. Then I march out of the store.

I *despise* Shredded Wheat.

• • • • •

By the time I get back to the hotel, the box of cereal is so soggy it's starting to fall apart. I dump it in a garbage bin outside the hotel. What a waste of fifteen cents!

The man in the gray uniform is still there, standing under the awning. He looks at me, but he doesn't make any move to open the door. So much for feeling like a queen. I guess a half-drowned kid doesn't rate.

I drip my way across the lobby. I'm not in the mood to read any more. It must be the shock of almost finding Grace. I feel as limp as a wrung-out dishrag. When I get to our room, I don't turn on the light because I'm afraid of waking Mom. I sit on the edge of the bed and eat a smushed cheese sandwich in the dark.

Then I put on my pajamas and crawl under the blankets. I stick my cold feet over to Mom's side of the bed. In two seconds, I am fast asleep.

Chapter Nineteen

"Where are you going?" I whisper.

Mom has opened the curtains a crack and the room is filled with pale gray light. She's dressed and she's fumbling in her purse.

"Out," Mom says. "For a walk."

I blink the sleep out of my eyes. "What time is it?"

"Four-thirty."

"I'm coming too."

I slip out of my pajamas and pull on a pair of shorts and a T-shirt. I lace up my running shoes.

We slip out of the hotel like thieves in the night. The lights are dim and there's no one around, not even the doorman. Outside, the sun isn't up yet, but the sky is pearly and a pale robin's egg blue. The lake is as smooth and calm as a sheet of glass.

Mom gazes all around. She takes a deep breath. "It's nice here."

"Really nice," I agree. I shiver a little. I should have brought a jacket.

"The mountains, the forest, the lake…this would be a nice place to grow up."

Mom's voice trembles. She's thinking about Grace. I squeeze her hand. "Come on," I say. "I'll show you the village."

We stroll along the path. Somewhere, some birds are singing like crazy. There's no one around. I love being out here with just my mom. It feels like we are the only people in the whole wide world who are awake. I tell that to Mom and she smiles and says that in China right now people are probably having dinner.

I'm thinking about that when voices drift across to us. I spot two men at the end of the red dock, loading boxes into a boat. Mom and I sit on a bench and watch them. One of the men waves and I wave back. Then the men climb into the boat and putt away, sending silver ripples across the water.

We sit on the bench for a long time, staring out at the lake and not talking. Then we start walking again. We go all the way to the gravel beach. A crow is hopping near the edge of the lake, holding a piece of bread in his beak. He flaps away when we get near. Mom sits on a log and I walk over to the pile of boards where those boys were playing yesterday. Some of the boards are nailed across two logs. It looks like they're building a raft. Nifty.

I look for flat rocks and try to skip them on the smooth water. My best is three skips. Then Mom and I cross over to the other side of the street and start walking back to the hotel.

All the businesses are closed up except for the Top Notch Café. The door is open and the smell of baking bread wafts out. "Smell that," Mom says, and she pokes her head in the door.

"We're not open yet," a voice calls out.

"Not even for a cup of coffee?" Mom says wistfully.

"Oh heck, you look cold. Come on in."

The woman speaking to us is behind a counter, sorting cutlery into piles. Mom and I sit at a table.

The woman brings over a steaming cup of coffee for Mom and a hot chocolate for me. She's a big heavy woman with the name *Daphne* stitched above her chest. "Fred could do you a fry up," she says. "Bacon, eggs, hash browns, and tomatoes."

"Heaven." Mom smiles.

When the food is ready, Daphne sets the heaped up plates in front of us and plops down in a chair at the next table. "Time to take a load off my feet. You're up with the birds, aren't you? You must be staying in one of them motor courts; or are you just passing through? Not that there's anywhere to pass through to, us being at the end of the road and all."

She pauses to take a breath.

"We're staying at the hotel," I say proudly.

Daphne raises her eyebrows. "Didn't take you for hotel guests. No offence, like. My niece Martha works at the hotel, a chambermaid you know, and she says they pay good and that it's ever so nice a place to work. You wouldn't believe what guests leave behind, not that she gets to keep anything, it all goes straight to the lost and found, an' she says the job is better than dishing up here at the Top Notch, which she did last summer. She's a hard worker an' all, was here from six in the morning 'til the supper gang left because she's saving her money to go to university."

She takes another breath and looks expectant, as if we're supposed to say something. Mom winks at me and murmurs, "University. That's impressive."

"First in the family. Gonna be a veter'narian." Daphne sticks out her hand. "I'm Daphne."

"Flora," Mom says. "And this is my daughter, Hope."

Daphne eyes my plate. "You're cleaning that up fast. Want some more hash browns?"

I control the urge to burp. "No, thank you."

"This is very kind of you to open early for us," Mom says.

Daphne shrugs. "Makes no never-you-mind to me. I'm here anyway. And it's nice to have someone to talk to. The hubby," Daphne jerks her head towards the kitchen, "he's baking that bread you smell and he don't say nothing 'til after lunch and then he don't say more than ten words. He don't start really talking 'til ten o'clock at night, and then I'm worn out and you can't shut him up."

Daphne heaves to her feet. "Time to make the coleslaw. I'll get you some more coffee and hot chocolate. You set here as long as you want. Two mites like you don't take up any space."

Mom sips her coffee slowly like she's not in a hurry to go anywhere. At seven, Daphne turns the sign around in the door so it says *Open*. The café fills up quickly, mostly with men in work clothes and muddy boots.

"Loggers," Daphne says as she scurries past with plates of food. "They know they can get a decent meal here."

And I mean *scurries*. For such a large woman, Daphne can move fast.

Mom watches her for a few minutes and then the next thing I know, she's up on her feet, getting the coffee pot from the counter and pouring coffee for the loggers.

My mouth drops open.

The loggers like Mom and she kind of flirts back with them, but I know it doesn't mean anything.

When the last one is gone and there's a lull, Mom pays our bill and Daphne says, "You can come anytime, Flora. You're good for business."

When we get out to the sidewalk, the sun is shining and the lake sparkles like it is made out of tiny diamonds.

Mom says, "That was fun. I haven't waitressed for years."

She sounds so happy. If only it would last.

Chapter Twenty

We end up having all our meals at the Top Notch Café. Mom says The Copper Room in the hotel is too expensive, but I think she likes hanging out with Daphne.

Granny would have said that Daphne could talk the hind end off a donkey. When the café is quiet, Daphne sits with us and chats. Over breakfast waffles, lunchtime bowls of homemade vegetable soup, and suppers of shepherd's pie, we hear all about the comings and goings of the village.

We hear about the post office lady who likes sherry, and shy Mrs. Wilkins who left her husband for an encyclopedia salesman, and Grandma Bell, who isn't really anyone's grandmother and who is losing her marbles, and Daphne's hubby Fred, who was born with one ear.

This is the best story of all and I'm dying to see Fred, but he stays hidden in the kitchen, banging pots and pans and sometimes hollering at Daphne.

When it's busy, Mom gets up and helps with the coffee or clears dirty dishes from the tables.

Daphne says she hates charging us, what with Mom being such a help, but Mom says we won't eat for free, so we get complimentary desserts: chocolate sundaes, apple pie à la mode (which is French and means with ice cream), and pineapple upside-down cake.

In between meals at the Top Notch, Mom shuts the curtains and lies down on the big bed in our room or sits on a bench across from the hotel, gazing at the lake. I borrow one of the bicycles from the hotel and ride around and around the village, hunting for Grace.

By the third day, I've about given up.

The bike is a pain in the you-know-where. One of the tires keeps going flat and I have to go to the gas station every few hours to get it pumped up. And the chain falls off unless I pedal really fast.

And there is no sign of Grace.

I make a loop, up along the main road beside the lake as far as the beach and then back on some of the little side roads, which are quiet and away from the lake and the tourists. I do this twenty times in a row.

The whole time, I'm thinking I might have made a big mistake about Grace. Maybe she and her great-aunt don't live in Harrison Hot Springs at all. Maybe they just come here every year on her birthday and have her picture taken.

There's one way we could find out. We could ask Daphne. You can bet she knows everyone in this village.

I suggest this over cheeseburgers at the Top Notch. Daphne is in the back talking to Fred and can't hear me, but I whisper anyway.

Mom says no. She doesn't want Grace to find out that people have been asking about her. She says it might scare her. She says there's a good chance Grace doesn't even know she's adopted.

That brings us to the big question. "If we find her, are we going to tell her who we are?" I ask Mom.

Mom doesn't answer me for a long time. "I don't know," she says finally.

• • • • •

When I'm not riding around on the bike looking for Grace, I swim in the outdoor pool or read my Nancy Drew books in the lounge. We came on Sunday, and by Thursday I've read both my books over again and I'm desperate for something new.

That's why I screech the bike to a halt, spraying gravel, when I spot a sign in the window of a brown building on one of the back roads. I've been pedaling pretty fast so the chain won't fall off, which is probably why I didn't notice it before. It says *Fraser Valley Regional Library*.

A bigger sign on the front of the building says *Harrison Hot Springs Municipal Hall*, which I think means that this is where the people who look after all the village's business work.

I lean my bike against a fence and go inside. There's a room with some tables and chairs, and a rack full of different colored pamphlets. A typewriter is clacking away through an open doorway. There's another door, closed, with a card tacked to it that says:

LIBRARY
Hrs. Mon-Thurs. 11:00 to 3:00

It's two o'clock on Thursday. I almost decided not to make that last loop on my bike because it's hot today, a gazillion degrees, and I don't want to miss the complimentary tea at the hotel. For once, luck is with me. If I hadn't gone around one more time and found the library today, I would have had to wait until next week.

I've never been to this kind of library before and I'm not

sure if you're supposed to knock, but in the end I just walk in.

The library is all in one room. There are some metal shelves crammed with books and a table with magazines and newspapers on it. A man is sitting at a desk. He smiles at me and says his name is Mr. Trout and is there anything he can help me with.

Of course I know that you're supposed to have a card to borrow books and that librarians are strict about that and can be very mean if you forget your card. But Mr. Trout looks nice and not mean at all.

I take a deep breath. "I'm staying at the hotel and I was wondering if I'd be allowed to borrow a book, just one, because I'm desperate and I promise to bring it back on Monday because I am a very, very fast reader."

Mr. Trout's eyes twinkle and I'm right, he is nice. He says, "You look like an honest person. I don't see why not. A weekend can be an eternity without anything to read. How about two books?"

He shows me where all the kids' books are at the back of the room. I always like to read the first three pages of a book before I decide to take it. Since I'm only picking two, I don't want to make a mistake, so it takes me awhile. A few people come in and out, but mostly it's just Mr. Trout and me.

I've narrowed it down to a mystery about a lost gold mine and *Old Yeller*, which I've read but want to read again. Mr. Trout is doing end-of-the-day kinds of stuff like tidying up the newspapers and magazines and rinsing his coffee mug at a sink beside the window. "I'm going to pop out to the post office," he says. "I'll just be a jiffy. You can hold the fort. We'll write down the titles of your books when I get back."

All librarians should be exactly like Mr. Trout. You can tell he really likes and trusts kids. I've never been in charge of a library before! Even if it's only for a few minutes.

I spot a chart on the wall covered with glittery gold stars and I walk over to have a closer look. At the top, it says *Harrison Summer Reading Club. Blast off to Reading!* There's a rocket on one side and a list of names. Beside each name are stars. A boy called David has the most, his row marches almost right across the chart.

I count his stars. Fifteen. I figure you get a star for every book you read. I could beat David hands down. I look over the other names. Cynthia's second. She has twelve stars. Most of the kids have five or six or seven stars.

There's only one kid with no stars. My heart stops *Bam!* when I read the name. Grace.

Chapter Twenty-One

I haven't exactly found Grace. But I've found her name, which is close.

I stare at the chart for a long time. Goosebumps pop up on my arms. Then I start to wonder what's happened to Mr. Trout. I take my books up to the desk and look for a piece of paper and a pen so I can write down the titles of my books.

His desk is cluttered with books, paper, cards, and tape. I rummage around for a pen and, under a stack of paper, I find a school exercise book with *Summer Reading Club* written on the front in black felt pen. I open it. On the first page is a handwritten list of names with addresses and phone numbers.

My heart pounds as I scan the list. There she is, a third of the way down. Grace Donnely. It's her, all right. Underneath her name, it says c/o Eve Williams. That must be her great-aunt.

By the time Mr. Trout calls out a cheery, "I'm back!" I've memorized the address: 56 Raven Road.

• • • • •

Raven Road is full of potholes and shaded by trees. I pedal past number 56 three times, faster than a speeding bullet so that I'll be a blur to anyone who might be looking out one of the windows. My library books bump up and down in the rickety wicker basket on the front of the bike.

Each time I whiz past, I gather a few more details.

I can only see part of the house because it's behind a tall overgrown hedge. It looks old. It's covered in gray-blue shingles. A cement walk with bushes smothered in pink roses on each side leads up to a front porch.

Whoosh! I blast by again.

There's a couch on the porch.

A tire hanging from a tree.

A lace curtain blowing out an upstairs window.

Fifth time. My legs are pumping. Sweat is trickling down my forehead because it's still so hot.

This time I slow down, but just a bit.

"Why do you keep going past my house?" a voice calls out from somewhere behind the hedge.

That distracts me.

BIG TIME.

So I don't see the cat until it streaks across the road, right in front of me. It's black and gold and longhaired. Holy Toledo! It's Jingle, come back to life!

I swerve to miss it. My front tire hits a pile of loose gravel. The bike sweeps out from under me and I crash to the ground.

My hands sting, there's dirt in my mouth, my right knee is on fire, and something warm is gushing down my leg. My instinct is to curl up in a ball and die. I moan and close my eyes.

"Are you all right?"

A girl with curly brown hair and blue eyes is standing beside me. She's wearing a red bathing suit. It's the girl in the photograph. It's Grace.

Cripes. This is not how I imagined I would meet my twin. Lying on the ground, dirty, sweaty, and bleeding to death.

"Are you all right?" she says again.

I can't get a single sound to come out of my mouth. Not even a squeak. I know that I'm gaping like a fish. I stand up slowly and clap my hand over my knee to try to stop the bleeding.

Grace picks up my bike. The chain is dragging on the ground. The library books have slid into the ditch, and she gets them and puts them back in the basket.

We both stare at my leg. There's a river of blood gushing through my fingers, all the way to my running shoe, which is turning red.

"You better come in and get some Band-Aids," Grace says.

She's going to think I have a serious talking problem if I don't say something.

I swallow. "Okay," I manage to mumble.

Grace wheels my bike to the side of the road and leans it against the hedge. I stumble after her, along the cement walk between the pink roses and up the steps onto the porch.

"On second thought, wait here," Grace says, looking at my dripping leg. "I'll be right back."

I glance around while she is gone. I can see the inside of the yard now, the part behind the hedge. It's a big square of grass that looks like it needs to be mowed. Half is shaded and half is in the sun. On the sunny side, there's a blue blanket with an open book lying on it.

Grace comes back with a wet cloth and a box of Band-Aids. I ease my hand off my knee and inspect the damage.

It's stopped bleeding, but there's an awful lot of gravel mushed into my skin. I dab at it, but that kills, so instead I scrub off the blood that's drying on my shin.

I stick four Band-Aids across my knee, crisscross. And a couple on the palms of my hands, which are scraped but not bleeding.

"By the way, I'm Grace Donnely," Grace says.

"Er, I'm Hope King."

Grace's face doesn't change at all. She's never heard of me.

"I'm staying at the hotel," I volunteer.

"Did you know you're shaking?" Grace says. "And you look awfully white. It could be shock. Maybe I should get you some water."

"I don't want to be a bother," I say.

"No problem," Grace says. "This is the most interesting thing that's happened all week." She sighs. "That just goes to show you how boring my summer is."

When Grace comes back with the water, she waits while I take a sip. Then she gives me what you could only call a penetrating look. "So why were you staring at my house?"

I get very busy with my glass of water. I can feel my cheeks turning hot.

"There's a hole in the hedge," she says. "I saw you go by. Five times."

"I was looking at *all* the houses," I say. "Not just yours. I like looking at houses."

I change the subject quickly. "What are you reading?"

"I wasn't reading," Grace says. "I was pretending to read. Actually, I was just working on my tan."

She pulls back a bathing suit strap to show me. I admire her tan line. She's much browner than me.

There's a tiny embarrassing silence.

If I can't think of something to say, I'll have to go and after all this trouble to find her, I *can't* go yet.

"Why were you pretending to read?" I say desperately.

Grace shrugs. "It's a deal I made with my aunt. If I get a star on this stupid chart at the library, then she'll take me to the Aga."

"What's the Aga?"

"The Aga Theater in Agassiz. *My Friend Flicka* is showing next week. I *have* to see it!"

Grace sighs. "She doesn't trust me so I have to write a book report. I'm doing this book called *Jane of Lantern Hill*. I've read the first chapter and the last chapter. But I need to know something that happens in the middle before I can write the stupid report."

"*Jane of Lantern Hill?*" I gasp. "That is my all-time favorite book!"

"Really?" Grace sounds like I've just admitted to liking

eating ants. "Nothing happens in it. At least in those two chapters."

"Nothing happens in it?" I'm practically screeching. "Jane goes to live with her father who she hasn't seen since she was a baby and they have this adorable house at Lantern Hill and she meets the Jimmy Johns and she captures an escaped lion and Jane just *hates* her Dad's sister Aunt Irene and I hate her too and…"

I stop for a breath. Yikes! I'm turning into Daphne.

Grace's mouth is hanging open, "Wow," she says. "You should write the book report for me."

We stare at each other.

Grace glances at her watch. "Darn, I have to get ready to go babysitting."

There's a glint in her blue eyes. "Are you doing anything tomorrow?"

Chapter Twenty-Two

Grace has Bible Camp in the morning. We arrange to meet at her house after lunch to work on the book report. I can't face wrestling with a greasy chain, so I wheel the bike back to the hotel.

All the way, this voice is screaming in my head. *You've found her! You've found Grace!*

To be honest, I'm a little shocked that she doesn't like to read. But who cares? There are a billion other things we're going to have in common.

I'm bursting to tell Mom about Grace, but she's out somewhere, probably having coffee with Daphne. I peel off the Band-Aids and soak in the bathtub until all the gravel has washed out of my knee. Then I fill the sink with water and scrub my bloody running shoe with a bar of soap.

The gift shop sells Band-Aids, so I buy a box from the lady with the pink glasses, who clucks over me like a mother hen. I sink into an armchair in the lounge and apply them like crazy. Then I hobble over to the tea table and load up a plate with chocolate chip cookies.

My wet running shoe makes a squelchy sound and feels yucky, my knee is stinging, and my shoulders are sunburnt. But I can't stop grinning.

Mom comes in just as I've finished eating.

I leap up without thinking, wince, and then limp over to meet her.

"I've been out walking," she says, smiling. "A cup of tea – "

"I've found her! I've found Grace! Mom, I *talked* to her!"

Mom's eyes grow as round as saucers. Then they turn glassy. Then she crumples to the floor in a dead faint.

The lady with the pink glasses rushes over from the gift shop. The doorman stops manning the door and sprints to Mom's side. Some guests gather around.

Everyone has suggestions. Get some water. Call a doctor. Give her room to breathe. I fly into a total panic. What if I've given Mom a stroke, like what happened to Granny?

In the middle of all this, Mom opens her eyes. She blinks a few times and everyone sighs with relief.

I would be mortified to be lying on the floor with a

bunch of people staring at me, but Mom is very dignified about the whole thing. The doorman helps her stand up and Mom thanks him and tells everyone that she is fine.

I hear a guest mutter, "Too much sun," and then the excitement is over and people go back to what they were doing.

Mom is swaying and she hangs onto my arm. I help her over to the couch by the fireplace and get her a cup of tea. Mom takes a long sip. She says, "Tell me everything."

I tell her *almost* everything. I don't tell her the part about me writing Grace's book report. It makes Grace sound, well, dishonest.

When I've finished, Mom frowns. "She was home by herself? Wasn't her aunt there?"

"I don't know," I say. "I never saw any aunt."

Mom's voice gets a little higher. "I don't like Grace being there by herself."

"Mom! She's eleven years old! I stay home by myself all the time."

"That's different," Mom says. "That's the city where's there's lots of people around. And you said she's going babysitting? She's too young to babysit."

"I would babysit too," I point out, "If I knew any babies."

This isn't going great. Finding Grace is supposed to make Mom feel better.

"Did she look too thin?" Mom says.

"No."

"Did she look happy?"

I think about how Grace's aunt is making her write a book report, which is way too much like school, and how Grace said her summer was so boring. I cross my fingers. "Yes."

"The polio…" Mom whispers.

"I couldn't really tell anything."

Mom finally relaxes.

"We'll go to The Copper Room for dinner tonight," she says. "We'll celebrate!"

•••••

Mom and I dress up. I wear my green dress. Mom says it makes me look older, like a teenager, but in a good way. Mom wears her blue dress, which is the exact color of her eyes.

A waiter shows us to a round table near the dance floor. A man with a pointy white beard is playing the piano, a man dressed entirely in black is playing an instrument that Mom whispers is a saxophone, and a woman with frizzy hair is singing.

We study the menu for ages. "Holy Toledo!" I gasp when

I see the prices, but Mom says firmly not to worry, this is a celebration. We order shrimp cocktails to start with, and roast beef. We're going to decide on desserts later. Mom has a glass of house wine and I have something called a Shirley Temple, which is pink and comes in a glass with a little paper umbrella.

A few couples are dancing. Mom taps her foot. I sip my Shirley Temple and look around. Most of the tables are full. I spot a man sitting by himself, reading his menu. It takes me a second to recognize him. It's Mr. Pinn!

"Granny's lawyer is over there," I tell Mom. "Mr. Pinn."

"Mr. Pinn?" Mom says. She sounds confused. "Here? Are you sure?"

"Right over there." I point and Mr. Pinn looks up at that exact moment. He waves. Then he gets up and makes his way to our table. He's wearing a gray-striped suit and a fancy purple polka-dot tie.

"Flora," he says. His face is bright red.

"Gerald," Mom says. "What a surprise."

Mr. Pinn turns even redder. "I've got a week's holidays and our conversations about Harrison Hot Springs made me realize how long it's been since I stayed here. So I thought, why not?"

"Why not?" Mom's face is red too. "Um, would you like to join us?"

"I'd be delighted! I'll just go back and get my glass of wine."

We watch him thread his way back to his table.

"He likes you," I say. "And he's quite good-looking."

"What?"

"He likes you. That's why he came here. It's obvious."

"No, he doesn't."

"Yes, he does."

"Doesn't," Mom hisses as Mr. Pinn comes back. A waiter brings an extra set of cutlery and Mr. Pinn insists on ordering a whole bottle of wine and another Shirley Temple for me. "Drinks are on me," he beams.

The wine is opened and tasted. I have never seen this done before. Mr. Pinn swishes it around in his mouth and looks thoughtful and then nods. Once it's poured, he says in a gallant voice, "Would you like to dance, Flora?"

Mr. Pinn is at least five inches shorter than Mom. He turns out to be a snappy dancer. He whirls Mom around the dance floor until she is breathless. Their feet fly. Mom's blue dress swirls; she looks gorgeous and everyone is staring at her.

By the time we've finished our roast beef, Mom and Mr. Pinn have danced five times. I've danced with Mr. Pinn twice. He told me exactly what to do, and it was easy! His polka-dot tie has come loose. He and Mom have polished off the bottle of wine. They're getting along like a house on fire. I'm not sure how I feel about this. The dancing was fun, but this is supposed to be *our* celebration. Mr. Pinn has butted in.

To my shock, halfway through our Baked Alaska desserts, Mom puts her fork down and tells Mr. Pinn about Grace. She tells him the whole story. Mr. Pinn hangs on every word, spellbound.

By the time she's finished, she's crying. "I'm a terrible mother," she gulps.

"Oh no," Mr. Pinn says. "No, no, no, no, no. Why, look at Hope here. She's a credit to you."

Mom wipes her eyes.

Mr. Pinn says, "We need a toast." He raises his wine glass. "To Grace."

Mom and I lift our glasses. Mom gives me a wobbly smile.

"To Grace."

Chapter Twenty-Three

"Not yet," Mom says. "I'm not ready."

It's the next day and Mom, Mr. Pinn, and I are having lunch at the Top Notch. We've been going around in circles for an hour, trying to figure out what to do.

These are the burning questions:

1. Does Grace know she was adopted?
2. Should I tell Grace that I'm her sister?
3. Should Mom meet Grace?

Mom twists her napkin into a knot. "I don't want to upset Grace. I don't want to turn her life upside down. I just want to know that she's happy and loved."

"Well, of course you do," Mr. Pinn says. "She's your daughter."

"I don't know what we should do," Mom practically wails. "We just kind of jumped into this without thinking it through."

"We need a strategy," Mr. Pinn says.

I notice the "we" right away. Since when did Mr. Pinn become part of this?

"This whole thing was a terrible idea," Mom moans.

I give Mom a cold look. If that's true, what was the big celebration last night all about? After all my detective work, not to mention hours of biking in the baking sun, I think Mom's being ungrateful.

"I don't think I ever really thought we'd find her," Mom confesses.

She takes a big breath. "I should talk to Grace's aunt first." Mom sounds kind of wild. "That would be the right thing to do. I could explain things."

"There's an idea," Mr. Pinn says. He looks pleased.

But I know Mom will never do that. There's this thing I've always known about Mom. She's terrible at doing things that are hard. Getting up in the morning and looking for a job. Going to Strawberry Teas with all the other mothers at my school. Now I can add talking to great-aunts and meeting her long-lost daughter to the list.

"Could you just play with her for a few days, Hope?" Mom pleads. "If she gets to know you first…"

"You mean, gets to know I'm a liar."

Mom's eyes well up with tears.

I mutter, "I'll try. But if you don't talk to her aunt soon, I'm going to tell Grace myself."

"Your mom just needs some time." Mr. Pinn reaches across the table and puts his hand on top of Mom's.

That makes me feel a little weird. They hardly know each other. And it's easy for Mom and Mr. Pinn not to worry. They aren't the ones who have to pretend to be someone else.

Chapter Twenty-Four

I've abandoned the bike. It's just too much trouble. And it only takes ten minutes to walk to Grace's house.

She's sitting on the porch in shorts and an orange sleeveless top, waiting for me. She wiggles over on the couch to make room. "Coast is clear," she says. "Aunty Eve has gone to Agassiz."

Grace is armed with a notebook and a pen. At the top of the page, she's written *Book Report for Jane of Lantern Hill*.

"Let's get this over with," Grace says.

I talk and Grace scribbles madly. I've still got plenty more to say, all about Jane baking her first pie, about her garden and her cats, when Grace puts her pen down. "Okay, that's good enough."

"But I'm not finished."

Grace yawns. "I am. I'm not writing a novel. This should satisfy the old bat." She grins at me. "You're a lifesaver. It was my lucky day when you crashed your bike."

My stomach clenches, waiting for Grace to ask me again why I was riding past her house. But she doesn't. "I've never met anyone who likes doing book reports," she says.

I don't want her to think I'm weird. I shrug. "I don't especially like doing book reports, I just like reading, that's all."

"Not me." Grace's blue eyes gleam. "You should join the reading club at the library. I bet you could beat David. He thinks he's so great, but he's actually an idiot."

I *could* beat him. He's read fifteen books and I can't remember how many books I've read this summer, but it's more than that. But when Grace mentioned the library before, I never said that I'd been there. Now I have to pretend that I don't know who David is.

"Why don't you join?" Grace persists.

"I'm not going to be here for very long."

"You're staying at the hotel, right?" Grace says. "Your whole family?"

I tense slightly. "Just me and my mom."

"Where's your dad?"

"I don't have a dad."

Grace looks interested. "Do you have any brothers or sisters?"

"No."

My voice comes out in a kind of croak, but Grace doesn't seem to notice. "Me neither," she says. "It's just me and Aunty Eve. My parents died in a car accident when I was five. That's when I moved here. I used to live in Vancouver."

"I live in Vancouver." My voice still isn't working right. I swallow a few times.

"Are you, like, on a holiday?"

"Sort of." *What if I told her? What if I told her right now?* I feel sick when I imagine the shocked look on her face.

"For how long?"

"I don't know," I mumble. "A few more days I guess."

Too many questions. I need to change the subject fast. "How was Bible Camp this morning?"

Grace heaves an enormous sigh. "Horrible, awful, boring. I'm the oldest one there. We sang a hundred million hymns and colored pictures like we were babies. Then we planted bean seeds in cups. I refused. How am I supposed to get excited about growing a bean?"

"Why do you go if it's so awful?" I say.

"I don't go because I want to. I'm *forced* to go. Aunty Eve makes me. What I want to do is go to a *real* camp. There's one in Sechelt and my best friends Janey and Louise are there right now. I *begged* to go."

Grace changes her voice so it's sharp and cross-sounding. "Why should I spend money to send you all the way to some fancy camp in Sechelt when there's a perfectly good camp right here in our village?"

"Your Aunty Eve said that?"

"Aunty *Evil*. That's what I'm calling her this summer. She doesn't get it. At a real camp, you get to canoe, sleep outside, have talent nights, and raid the boys' cabins. Janey and Louise got to go last year too. They said it was a scream. Wouldn't you just love that?"

"I don't know," I say honestly. Camp sounds terrifying to me. I bet there's nowhere to escape from popular kids and just read a book or something.

Grace sighs. "Oh well. This is the last week of Bible Camp and then the torture is over. And then, in one more week, Janey and Louise will be back. They are my *absolute* best friends. They just about died when Aunty Eve said I couldn't go with them. They were going to go on strike and stay home too, but their parents had already paid for it and everything, so they had to go."

I feel a sharp pang of envy. I can't imagine having two absolute best friends who would go on strike and give up camp just for me. To be honest, I can't imagine having any best friends at all. I never have. It's one more thing besides loving books that's different between Grace and me. This is stupid and makes no sense at all but I've decided not to like Janey and Louise. I'm glad they're away.

Grace's legs were curled underneath her, but now she stretches them out. "God, my legs are hairy," she moans.

I stare at Grace's legs, which actually are quite hairy. A hot flush spreads across my cheeks.

Grace's right leg is way skinnier than her left leg, and it kind of curves towards her foot. It's the first time I've noticed it.

It must be the polio. It hits me full blast then, that this whole thing is not just some made-up story in a book. I really do have a twin sister and she's sitting beside me, *right beside me*, and my mother gave her away because she had polio.

Don't stare, a voice whispers in my head.

And then, *Tell her, you have to tell her*.

"Are you allowed to shave?"

"What?" I struggle to pull my thoughts together. Grace's skinny leg has totally flustered me.

"Does your mom let you shave your legs?"

"I don't know. I've never asked."

The truth is, I've never worried about hair on my legs. I inspect them now. They're not nearly as bad as Grace's (one more thing that's different about us), but they're definitely hairy. How did I miss that before? I have so many things to worry about and now I have to add hairy legs to my list.

"I'm not allowed," Grace says. "Aunty Evil has a fit if I even mention it. She says it's vain to worry about hairy legs when you're eleven years old."

She jumps up. "Can you keep a secret?"

"Yeah."

I mean, aren't I keeping the biggest secret of all? I get this crazy urge to burst into hysterical laughter, even though it's not one bit funny.

"Come on."

Grace pushes open the screen door and I follow her inside her house. After being out in the bright sun, it's dark inside. We walk down a long narrow hallway, past a kitchen and a living room, and then up a flight of stairs.

As I walk behind her, I try to decide if she's walking normally. She doesn't really look like she's limping, but it's hard to tell. She certainly has no trouble climbing up the stairs.

"This is my room," Grace says.

The room is tiny. There's a bed with a yellow bedspread and with a mound of stuffed animals on the pillow, and a blue dresser and a desk by the window. The window is open and a lace curtain is blowing in the breeze. I can smell something sweet like flowers. The floor is buried under heaps of clothes.

"It's a mess," Grace says cheerfully. "I'm not allowed to go anywhere until I clean it up or else I'll be grounded."

I'm only half-listening to Grace. My eyes are riveted on the stuffed animals. There's a monkey, a dog, a teddy bear, a rabbit, and a hippo. My heart skips a beat. It's my hippo, Harry. The same pinkish fur and black button eyes.

It's Harry all right, but it can't be.

Chapter Twenty-Five

I pick up the hippo. "Where did you get this?"

"That old hippo?" Grace shrugs. "I don't know. I've always had it."

"Did someone give it to you?"

"I told you, I've always had it." Grace is looking at me like I've lost my marbles. "My mom must have given it to me when I was little. I think she gave me all these stuffed animals."

"Your mom?" I say, confused.

And then I get what Grace means. Her adopted mom, the nurse Sharon.

How can I tell Grace that she's wrong? That I don't think it was Sharon who gave her the hippo. That I'm positive it was Granny. Granny told me that when I was two, she and Grandpa went on a cruise to Alaska and they bought Harry in a gift shop in one of the little towns they stopped in. Granny didn't tell me the whole truth. She must have bought two hippos.

Grace opens her top drawer and pulls out a piece of newspaper. She hands it to me, "Look at this."

I read it out loud:

Ladies: Read This!
Unwanted hair removed permanently from face, arms,
and legs, with Egyptian misopile. Harmless – leaves
skin soft and smooth. Egyptian misopile is a liquid and
is applied directly from the bottle.
Money back guarantee.
$3.00 per bottle
Fortune Products
1176 Sherbrooke West
Montreal, Quebec.

By the time I get to the last line, we are both giggling like hyenas.

"I sent away for it," Grace says. "It might even come today. The mail will be sorted by now, so I gotta go to the post office before Aunty Eve gets there. She'll kill me if she finds out I ordered this." She grins. "But at least I won't have hairy legs in my coffin!"

This makes us screech with laughter again.

Grace kicks at a mound of clothes. "I'll do this later. Aunty Eve won't be back for ages. She'll never know if I go out. Come on!"

If Janey and Louise were here, would Grace want to be with me? I guess she's desperate for someone to hang around with. I push that thought away and follow Grace downstairs. She's a little bit slower going down and she's holding onto the rail with one hand.

"You didn't bring your bike," Grace says when we get outside.

"It's the hotel's and it doesn't work that well," I say. I add uncertainly, "If you want to bike, that's okay; I can walk fast."

"I don't have a bike," Grace says. "I can't ride one. My leg gets too tired."

I freeze.

"I had polio when I was little," Grace says. "It made my leg gimpy."

Grace sounds like it's no big deal. I can't think of anything to say. Not one thing. Finally, I stammer, "Does it hurt?"

"Not really any more. It used to hurt a lot. Sometimes it aches, but mostly it just gets too weak to do stuff."

"Oh."

Grace doesn't have any trouble talking about herself. Not like me. I'm a pro at hiding stuff. I can't believe how she can just rattle on. As we walk along the shady streets, she tells me more about the polio. She tells me how she used to wear leg braces and how when she moved to Harrison Hot Springs, the kids at school thought she was contagious.

"David was the worst. He has this gang of horrible boys he hangs around with, but he's the worst. He told everyone not to play with me. That I would give them polio germs."

"That's awful," I gasp.

"It *was* awful. But then I met Janey and Louise. And we instantly became best friends."

When we get to the post office, we go inside and Grace takes a silver key out of her pocket. She opens a box in the middle of a wall of mailboxes. "Nothing," she says, crouching down so she can see right inside. "Darn!"

A man is sorting parcels behind a counter at one end of the post office. "Hi there, Grace!" he calls out.

"Anything for me?" Grace says, sounding hopeful.

"Just a sec." The man looks at the last few parcels. "Nope. Not today."

"Double darn," Grace sighs.

"When are your partners in crime getting back from camp?" the man asks.

"One more week."

"Here." The man slips Grace two quarters. "It's a scorcher today. Buy yourself and your friend an ice cream."

Grace says that the Top Notch has the best ice cream. I hold my breath when we go inside, praying that Mom won't be there. She's not. We order double cones, but Daphne gives us each an extra scoop. I know right away that I want chocolate, but Grace takes ages to choose. This is a perfect time to test our mental telepathy. While Grace is flitting back and forth, peering in the tubs, I concentrate as hard as I can.

Strawberry. Make her choose strawberry.

Choose strawberry.

Choose strawberry.

Choose strawberry.

"Butterscotch," Grace says.

Cripes.

While Daphne is scooping out Grace's cone, I keep my eyes peeled on the doorway into the kitchen. I still haven't seen Fred with the one ear.

We take our cones outside and sit on a bench beside the lake and look at all the boats while we eat. Three boys walk by and one of them, a boy with black hair and a dark tan, makes a rude oinking noise like a pig.

"You just wish you had one," Grace retorts. "Mmmm, this is soooo delicious."

"Oink! Oink!"

"That's David," Grace says when they're gone. "Me and Janey and Louise hate him."

David is one of the boys I saw working on the raft at the beach. I tell Grace and she looks very interested. "A raft! I didn't think David was smart enough to think of something cool like that."

Grace attacks her cone in big gulps and I lick slowly. I'm still polishing off the last bits of mine when we walk back to her house.

By the time we get there, Grace is limping a little. She's also complaining about how hot she is. "I'll make us some Kool-Aid," she says. "Then I'd better clean up my room."

She slams to a stop at the end of the walk in front of her house. "Uh-oh."

A figure is standing on the porch. My first impression is *gray*. Gray stockings, gray dress, gray hair pulled back in a tight bun.

"Aunty Eve, you're back early," Grace says. "This is my new friend Hope. She's staying at the hotel. We've just been to the post office so you wouldn't have to go in this heat."

I wish I wasn't holding the end of this ice-cream cone. I wish there wasn't a blob of butterscotch ice cream on Grace's chin.

Aunty Eve gives me a cool look. Up close, she's very tall. And thin. She reminds me of a heron I saw once on the beach in Vancouver. Even her eyes are gray, like the ocean on a cloudy day. They are not smiley eyes. "Run along, Hope," she says in an icy voice.

She turns to Grace. "And you, young lady. Inside. Now."

Chapter Twenty-Six

I make it all the way to dessert before I blow up. It's Daphne's famous chocolate pie and it's wrecked for me because I'm so mad. Ever since we sat down, Mom's been firing questions at me. I've only known Grace one day and I'm supposed to be an expert on her. How should I know what her favorite color is? Or if she likes dogs? Or what kind of grades she gets at school?

We all ordered fish and chips. I noticed Mr. Pinn ate every scrap, mopping up his ketchup with his last few fries, but Mom hardly had a bite. She was too busy interrogating me like the FBI.

Now we're at dessert and my mouthful of creamy

chocolate pie sticks in my throat. I swallow and then explode. "I'M NOT A SPY!"

"Don't be silly," Mom says.

"That's what it feels like." I lower my voice because a girl at another table is staring at me.

I hate this. I'm not exactly lying to Grace, but I'm hiding stuff and that makes me feel horrible. And the longer it goes, the worse it's going to get.

"You're making me into a spy," I repeat. "I thought you were going to talk to her aunt."

"I haven't decided," Mom says.

"Because you don't have the guts," I practically hiss. "Just like you don't have the guts to admit what you did to Grace. That you gave her away like she was worth nothing."

Mom turns white. She clamps her lips together.

I hate fighting with Mom. But I hate what she is making me do even more.

I ignore an annoying voice in my head that reminds me: *This whole thing was your idea.*

I just didn't think it was going to be like this. The truth is, I didn't really think about what was going to happen. I push my pie away.

I'm ready to pounce on Mr. Pinn if he says anything, anything at all, to defend Mom. But he's gobbling up his chocolate pie and he keeps his eyes on his plate.

• • • • •

After supper, Mom and Mr. Pinn and I walk along the path that goes past the hotel, away from the village. I wasn't going to go, but at the last minute I change my mind. There's nothing else to do. The lake is on one side and a steep forested hillside is on the other. Mom and Mr. Pinn are holding hands. Cripes. What does that mean? Mom is talking to Mr. Pinn, but she hasn't said one word to me. She's still hurt or angry or something.

After about ten minutes, we come to a small fenced enclosure. There's a square pool inside, like a well, deep and dark and smelly.

"What's that?" I say.

"The hot springs," Mr. Pinn says. "They pipe the water from here to the pool. It's very therapeutic."

"What does therapeutic mean?" I say.

"That it's good for you. People have been coming to Harrison for the water since the 1800s, when the hot springs were discovered. The story is that some miners were coming back from the gold rush. They were half frozen to death and decided to land on the shore of the lake and build a fire. One of the miners stood up in the canoe and fell in. To his surprise, the water was hot. He called his buddies to come and join him. They warmed up in the water, then built their fire, ate some baked beans, and continued on their way. The rest is, as they say, history."

"Is that true?" I look around. It might have happened right here.

"Maybe," Mr. Pinn says. "It's a good story, anyway. And it's true that people have been coming to Harrison for almost a hundred years to partake of the healing waters." This is probably the longest, most interesting conversation Mr. Pinn and I have had. He's really not so bad. Even if he uses words like *partake*.

Healing. I think about that as we walk back to the hotel.

It's what Mom needs. To heal. Maybe it was a good idea to come here after all. But she seems to be getting worse, not better. I wish I could take back what I said at supper. But it's too late.

• • • • •

I don't want to go inside yet. I tell Mom that I'm going to walk around the village for a while. She gives me this look that's kind of sad and mad at the same time and says, "Don't stay out once it gets dark."

I don't really think about where to go. I just wander, mixing in with the tourists. My stomach is in a knot. How am I going to tell Mom that Aunty Eve is mean?

Aunty Eve is so different from Mom. Mom wouldn't make me go to Bible Camp if I didn't want to. And she doesn't care a wit if my bedroom is messy (I don't even have a bedroom right now, but that's beside the point.) And Mom trusts me. She would never make me write a book report just to prove that I'd read a book. She'd *believe* me. And I bet she'd let me shave my legs if I really wanted to.

When you add it all up, Aunty Eve really is Aunty Evil. What if I tell Mom? For a second, I imagine her rushing in like a knight on a white horse to save Grace from the witch. Kidnapping her and taking her home with us. And everyone living happily ever after.

Wait a sec. This is Mom I'm talking about. She doesn't do white knight stuff. If she finds out what Aunty Eve is like, she'll feel so bad about Grace that she'll probably crawl into bed and never get up again. And then my whole plan to find Grace will have totally backfired.

Without realizing it, I've come to the end of Grace's street. I walk past her house. My stomach tightens. What if Grace has been grounded for sneaking out without cleaning up her messy room? What if I never see her again? I've just found my sister. I can't lose her now.

I stare up at the house. Grace's bedroom window is at the front, wide open, with the lace curtains pulled back. Grace is leaning on the sill, looking out. She waves when she sees me and yells, "I'll be right down!"

I wait on the porch and she appears in a moment, banging the screen door behind her. We flop down on the couch.

"Is your aunt here?" I ask nervously. I'm praying she's out somewhere. Aunty Eve is scary.

"She's at the chapel," Grace says. "There's some missionary woman showing slides of Africa."

"Did you get in big trouble?"

"Grounded." Grace doesn't sound too upset. She sticks her good leg out and spins her bare foot in circles. She's painted her toe nails bright red since this afternoon.

"For how long?"

Grace shrugs. "I don't know. I bet I'll still have to go to Bible Camp tomorrow, which is very unfair. Don't you think if you're grounded, you should be grounded for everything? Not just the good things?"

"I guess so. I've never been grounded."

"Really? I've been grounded *millions* of times."

Just then, the orange and black cat that looks like Jingle pops through a rose bush at the end of the walk. He saunters towards us. Something is dangling from his mouth.

"It's a mouse!" Grace squeals. "Don't bring it here, Tiki!"

The cat veers onto the grass and hunches under a bush.

"That's Tiki," Grace says. "He's Mrs. Jordan's cat. He lives next door."

We watch Tiki devour the mouse. "It's disgusting when he does that," Grace says. "But he's actually quite a nice cat. He's a Persian."

"He's gorgeous." I still can't believe how much he looks like Jingle.

"I used to have a cat that looked just like Tiki," Grace says suddenly. "At least I think I did. It's so weird. Whenever I see Tiki, I remember this other cat. I have this picture inside my head of myself petting it when I was just a little kid."

I stare at Grace. "What was its name?"

"I don't know. I asked Aunty Eve if I had a cat when I lived in Vancouver with my mom and dad, but she says I didn't. She says my mom was allergic to cats. So maybe it's just something that I made up."

I'm shaking. Grace didn't make it up. She's remembering Jingle. I want to tell her, but I can't. I feel miserable again about this whole big secret.

Tiki abandons the remains of his mouse, strolls over to the walk, and disappears back into the rose bushes.

Grace jumps up. "I've been thinking about David's raft. I'm going to go take a look at it. See if it's any good."

"Now? You're grounded."

Grace grins. "I'm safe for awhile. The Africa slides will take ages, and there'll be tea and cake afterwards. I can get down to the beach and back and Aunty Eve will never find out. You want to come?"

I can't believe Grace would take that chance. But I don't want to miss out on anything. "Sure."

I wait while Grace goes inside for her sandals.

Then we set out for the lake. We have to walk right past the chapel where the missionary is showing her slides. The door is propped open and applause spills out from inside.

"It sounds like it's over. Maybe we should go back." I'm scared stiff about Aunty Eve catching Grace.

"Everyone will want to ask tons of questions," Grace says. "And then they have to eat and have their tea. That'll take forever. Trust me. I've got lots of time."

There are quite a few people strolling along the path beside the lake, but the little beach is deserted. The raft is pulled up on the gravel, away from the water. It's made out of two skinny logs with old boards nailed across. Some of the boards are crooked and there are gaps between them.

Grace stares at it for a minute without saying anything.

"It looks pretty good," I say.

"Not bad," Grace grunts. But she looks impressed. "It probably floats okay. How many boys did you say were working on it?"

"David, and two others."

"Harry and Sam, David's best friends, I bet," Grace says.

She picks up the end of a long pole resting across the raft. "This must be for pushing it along. I'd give anything to try it."

Just then, something clatters against the end of one of the logs.

A rock.

Then another one, zinging right past my ear.

Holy Toledo!

"Look out!" Grace cries.

I duck, terrified.

"HEY!" a voice hollers. "GET AWAY FROM THERE!"

Grace and I spin around. David is charging across the beach towards us, his arm raised, ready to hurl another rock.

"WHAT DO YOU THINK YOU'RE DOING? DON'T TOUCH THAT! GET AWAY!" he yells.

He's close enough now for me to see that his face under his tan is red and his eyes are flashing with fury.

My heart leaps into my throat.

"PUT THAT ROCK DOWN, YOU MANIAC!" Grace screams back. "ARE YOU CRAZY?"

David hesitates. Then he drops the rock. He sticks his chin out. "Stay away from my raft!" he growls.

"You could have killed us!" Grace says in a shrill voice.

"With a rock? Right. Ooooo, I'm so scared of a teeny little rock. What are you going to do? Tell your aunty?"

"Shut up!" Grace screeches.

David narrows his eyes until they are slits. "Now get out of here."

"Ha! You don't own this beach. Is there a sign somewhere that says we can't stand here if we want? I don't see any sign. Do you, Hope?"

"No," I gulp.

"I own the raft," David spits back. "And there's no girls allowed."

"Oh. So that's what this is supposed to be? A raft? Really? You sure can't tell."

"Very funny. It's a lot better than you could make."

"If I wanted to make a raft, which I *don't*, at least I'd make something that wasn't going to fall apart."

David and Grace glare at each other.

Then Grace says in a loud voice, "Come on, Hope. We've got better things to do than stand around here looking at this pile of junk."

Grace marches back towards the road, her head held high. I follow her, my heart thudding.

Partway, she turns and shouts over her shoulder, "AND I WOULDN'T USE ROTTEN BOARDS!"

Chapter Twenty-Seven

When we get to the chapel, people are standing outside on the sidewalk, chatting in little groups. I spot the tall straight back of Aunty Eve, who towers over everyone else. She's facing away from us.

Grace must see her too. "Walk faster," she hisses.

Grace is limping a lot by the time we get to her house. We go into the kitchen, pour ourselves glasses of cherry Kool-Aid, and bring them out to the porch.

We've only been back eight minutes, max, when Aunty Eve arrives.

Too late, I realize that I don't really know how being grounded works. I panic that Grace is going to get in trouble because I'm here. I'm ready to flee.

Aunty Eve frowns, and she seems to look at me extra hard, but she just says, "Hello, Hope."

"Hello," I say.

"How was the slide show?" Grace asks.

"Inspiring," Aunty Eve says.

"Great!" Grace says.

"Mrs. Gillingham was there."

"Oh."

I have no idea who Mrs. Gillingham is, but I have a horrible feeling this means trouble.

"I asked her if you were behaving at Bible Camp. If you were helping out with the younger children and setting a good example."

"Oh," Grace says again.

"I was extremely disappointed to hear the exact opposite. That you're not participating at all." Aunty Eve looks grim. "I'd be interested to know what you have to say."

Grace studies her red toenails. I don't think she has anything to say.

"Mrs. Gillingham is going to a lot of work to make Bible Camp exciting," Aunty Eve says.

"Planting beans?" Grace mutters.

"Pardon me?"

"Nothing."

"Since you're apparently wasting everyone's time," Aunty Eve continues, "I've decided to pull you out."

Grace looks up. Her eyes shine. "Really? Oh, thank you, thank you, thank you. I promise I –"

"You can help me with the pies tomorrow instead," Aunty Eve says. "I have a huge order. Forty-three."

I'm positive I see a tiny smile flicker across her face. "We'll start extra early because it's going to be hot. Five more minutes and then I want you to get ready for bed."

"Now?" Grace says. "It's only eight o'clock. And it's roller-skating tonight!"

"Roller-skating will have to wait until next week." Without another word, Aunty Eve sails inside the house.

"Every Tuesday night they have roller-skating at the community hall," Grace says with a huge sigh. "It's so much fun."

"I'm a good roller-skater," I say, and then I worry that I sound like I'm bragging. "Well, not *that* good."

"I'm terrible," Grace says. "I can only go in one direction and my leg gets tired really fast. But I love it."

We sit quietly for a moment.

Then I ask, "*Forty-three* pies?"

"They're for the logging camps. Aunty Eve makes pies for them every week." Grace groans. "Forty-three! It's gonna take all day!"

She slumps back into the couch. "Pie Day. It's a fate worse than death. And no roller-skating! Aunty Eve is trying to torture me. I knew it! I should have planted those stupid beans!"

•••••

When I get back to the hotel, I change into my bathing suit and go to the pool. I practice my tuck turns for a while, but some guests who are soaking in the shallow end glare at me. I guess it's because I'm making little waves, and people come to this pool to relax.

And heal.

That makes me think of Mom, but that makes me feel sad so I decide to think about something else instead.

I float on my back and think about pies.

I've never made a pie, but it can't be all that hard.

By the time the man comes to tell everyone that the pool is closed for the night, I've made up my mind.

Fifteen minutes later, I crawl into bed beside Mom.

"You smell like a swimming pool," she murmurs, half asleep.

Mom's been getting up early in the mornings to help Daphne with the breakfast crowd. "Will you wake me up when you go to the café?" I say.

"Mmmm," Mom says. "Why?"

I wriggle deeper into the blankets. "It's Pie Day tomorrow," I say. "I don't want to be late."

Chapter Twenty-Eight

Mom and I sleep in. The Top Notch is humming by the time we get there, almost all the tables filled with loggers and sleepy tourists.

Mom pours her own coffee and we sit at a table in the corner.

"Morning, Sunshine," Daphne says to me as she bustles past with two plates of eggs and bacon. "Fred's put his strawberry pancakes on special today. Buttermilk. Plenty of whipped cream."

They sound yummy, but I'm in a hurry. "Just some corn flakes, please, Daphne."

I shovel in my cereal and say good-bye to Mom, who's finished her coffee and is up at the counter making a fresh pot. I'm at Grace's house in five minutes. A tantalizing smell, like a bakery, drifts through the open front door and down the walk.

I hear Grace call out, "It's Hope!"

Grace and Aunty Eve are on the porch. Aunty Eve is sitting in the middle of the couch. Grace is propped up against a pillow at one end, her bare legs draped across Aunty Eve's lap. Aunty Eve is rubbing Grace's skinny right leg. Aunty Eve's hands are big like a man's and tanned. There's a bottle of pale purple liquid on the floor beside them.

"Good morning, Hope," Aunty Eve says. She looks right at me and I get the feeling that there's something else she wants to say, but she doesn't. She picks up the bottle and pours some liquid into her hand. Over the smell of pie, I smell something new, like flowers.

"What's that?" I ask.

"Lavender oil," Aunty Eve says. She massages Grace's leg. Up and down, up and down. Her hands look strong and gentle at the same time.

"We've got four peach pies in the oven," Grace says. "And four more baking at Mrs. Jordan's next door."

I sit down on the top step. "Am I too late to help?"

"Not at all," Aunty Eve says. "We're just taking a little break. There's lots more to do."

She puts the lid on the bottle of lavender oil and says, "How does that feel now, Grace? Not so achy?"

"Better," Grace says, sitting up.

"You girls can clean the blueberries for me," Aunty Eve says. "Thank you for coming, Hope. Many hands make light work."

"That's what my granny used to say!"

"Indeed." Aunty Eve actually smiles. "Grandmothers are very wise."

I get this sudden surprising thought that Granny and Aunty Eve would have liked each other, which doesn't make any sense at all. Aunty Eve is mean.

• • • • •

The kitchen is way bigger than the kitchen in our apartment. There's a big black wood stove at one end. Holy Toledo! It must be a hundred degrees in here.

It's bright with big windows, all open wide, and rows of leafy green plants in little pots on the sills. A long counter is dusted with flour and cluttered with baking things: mixing bowls, pie plates, a bag of sugar, a sack of flour, measuring cups, and a huge wooden rolling pin.

There are four crates of blueberries on a long wooden table. Grace and I sit on chairs. We have to sort through the berries, putting them into bowls, picking out leaves and bits of sticks.

When Aunty Eve isn't looking, we sneak blueberries. They're fat and sweet and they kind of pop in your mouth. Scrumptious!

Grace gets bored quickly. She bangs her feet against her chair and sighs a lot. But I like it.

When all the berries are clean, Aunty Eve shows me how to weave strips of pastry across the tops of the pies. At first, my strips keep breaking, but soon I get the hang of it. Grace is already pretty good at it. She also knows how to use a fork to do something Aunty Eve calls "crimping the edges."

One by one, the pies come out of the oven in the wood-stove, brown and crusted with sugar and cinnamon, with blueberry juice oozing out the sides. There isn't room for all the pies in the kitchen. Soon they are cooling on wire racks all over the house: in the living room, the pantry, even the bathroom!

Grace and I take some of the pies next door to bake. Mrs. Jordan is a frizzy-haired woman wearing a dressing gown, even though it's the middle of the day! She's on her porch reading magazines and smoking cigarettes. I think it's unfair that she doesn't offer to help make the pies. I bend down to pat Tiki, who is stretched out on his tummy in a patch of sun.

By two o'clock, the last pie is in the oven. Forty-three pies for the logging camps, one blueberry pie for Mrs. Jordan, and one peach pie and one blueberry pie for Grace and Aunty Eve.

Aunty Eve fixes us a tray with bread and butter, hard-boiled eggs, glasses of icy milk, and huge pieces of warm blueberry pie.

Grace says she'd like to try the peach pie too, but Aunty Eve says that two pieces of pie is gluttony. She hands Grace the tray and says, "Take this outside into the shade."

We sit on Grace's sun tanning blanket, which we drag into the shade of a huge leafy tree. We're both starving and we gobble up the bread and eggs. The pie is divine, each warm, sugary, sticky, melt-in-your-mouth bite. When we're finished, we have blue smiles and white milk moustaches.

Grace goes inside and comes back with her nail polish. She paints my toe nails bright red to match hers. We stretch our legs out, side by side, and admire the effect. Grace's feet are narrow and dainty, mine wide and square. Then we paint our fingernails. We dangle them in the sun to dry.

The screen door bangs. Aunty Eve crosses the grass towards us.

Grace flashes her fingers at Aunty Eve. "What do you think?"

"I think," Aunty Eve says with a sniff, "that it makes you look cheap."

She sniffs again. "Like a chorus girl."

I hide my hands in my lap.

Aunty Eve gives Grace a folded dollar bill. "Right now, I want you to go to Inkman's and pick up a box of cornstarch and some raisins."

She bends over and picks up the tray. "Mrs. Stratton has invited us for dinner tonight. So don't dawdle. You need to have a bath and wash your hair."

Grace groans. "It's boring at the Strattons'. They're *old*. I'll be the only kid and there's nothing to do there and – "

"I'd like you to stop for the mail on your way back," Aunty Eve says.

"The mail." Grace perks up instantly. "Sure thing."

• • • • •

We go to the post office first. There's no hair removal package waiting for Grace. There's a letter, though, in a pale blue envelope with Grace's name in very curly handwriting and little hearts in the corners.

"It's from Louise and Janey," Grace yelps.

She tears open the envelope and reads bits of the letter to me as we walk to Inkman's. There's a long part about going on a hike through a swamp, which I think sounds like a nightmare.

Grace sighs. "I wish I was there! It's so unfair!"

At Inkman's, Grace pays for the cornstarch and raisins. I have most of the dollar Mom gave me left. I pick out a giant jawbreaker, my favorite. I tell Grace I'll buy her one too.

Turns out, Grace hates jawbreakers. She chooses a peppermint stick instead.

I hate peppermint.

Cripes.

Is there *anything* about us that's the same?

We stand outside on the sidewalk and suck on our candy.

Grace takes her peppermint stick out of her mouth. "I think we should try out that raft."

"Now?" It comes out kind of garbled and I spit out the jawbreaker into my hand. "I thought you had to go out for dinner."

"I mean tomorrow. Really, really early in the morning. Before David gets up. He'll never know."

I can still feel that rock zinging past my cheek. "I'm not sure," I say slowly.

"Come on." Grace's eyes gleam. "I want to see if it floats. It's not fair that Louise and Janey are having all the fun. We have to have some fun, too."

Something tells me this is a bad idea. A very bad idea. David is the fiercest boy I've ever met. And how can Grace be totally sure what time he gets up? What if he catches us? But I hear myself say, "Okay."

"Get up really early and come to my house," Grace says. "Like around six o'clock. I'll be ready."

I can see lots of problems. We don't have an alarm clock. Usually Mom gets up early to go to the café and that wakes me up too. But look what happened this morning. We slept in! And I'll have to sneak out because I think this raft might be one of those things that mothers have fits about.

My jawbreaker is turning the palm of my hand black. Before I pop it back into my mouth, I say, "I'll try."

Chapter Twenty-Nine

"Goin' to be a storm tonight," Daphne says. "A dandy by the looks of that sky."

I look out the café window. The sky is still blue, but far away over the mountains, black clouds are piling up.

Daphne lowers herself into a chair with a cup of coffee. Mom, Mr. Pinn, and I are eating buttermilk biscuits, crispy fried chicken, and potato salad.

"Dead in here today," Daphne says. "Happens sometimes. Don't matter. We're expecting a big party for breakfast tomorrow at eight. They phoned ahead. Fred's goin' to make Eggs Benedict."

"I'll help," Mom promises.

"Do you get bad storms on the lake?" Mr. Pinn says.

"You bet. And they can come up fast. Rain like there's no tomorrow. And wind. Why, I remember a few years ago, waves were so high we lost six boats. Broke loose from the dock and…"

Daphne is off and running. I only half-listen.

I'm praying there's a great big storm. A storm to beat all records. A storm that washes David's raft clear away.

•••••

Mom and I leave our window open because it's muggy. As soon as we get in bed, I close my eyes and pretend to be asleep. I don't want to talk about Grace. Mom sighs and turns over, and in a few minutes she's snoring.

I'm in the middle of a dream about a pie-eating contest when a crash wakes me up. Thunder! Holy Toledo! It sounds like it's right on top of the hotel.

How can Mom sleep through that? I crawl out of bed and stumble to the bathroom. I look at Mom's watch, which is beside the sink. Three o'clock.

I slide back under the covers. I decide to stay awake until it's time to get up.

Each boom of thunder makes my heart jump. Gradually it sounds farther away. There's a new sound now, coming through the open window. Pounding rain.

The next thing I know, my eyes pop open, it's light in the room, and Mom is standing by the window, dressed.

"What time is it?" I mumble.

"Six o'clock," Mom says. "Storm's over. It looks like it poured."

"Is it still raining?" I say hopefully.

"It's stopped. There's a bit of blue sky peeking through. But it's windy out there. The lake is pretty choppy."

She bends over the bed and gives me a kiss. "I'm going to the Top Notch. You go back to sleep."

"Okay," I say.

Somehow I don't think a bit of wind is going to stop Grace. I count to five hundred. Then I hop out of bed and pull on my shorts, T-shirt, and running shoes.

I dodge rain puddles all the way to Grace's house.

• • • • •

Grace is huddled on the couch on the porch, wrapped up in a patchwork quilt.

"Aunty Eve?" I say nervously.

"Fast asleep," Grace says.

She pulls off the quilt and jumps up. "I thought you'd never get here. Let's go!"

All the way to the beach, Grace chatters about the storm. I keep my eyes peeled for David. A person can't be too careful. But the streets are empty.

It's cooler by the lake and the wind is much stronger. Far out on the water, I can see white caps. But closer to shore, the water is pretty calm and I think it will be okay. It's not like we're going out far because we can only go as deep as the pole will reach.

I hug my arms to my chest while Grace walks around the raft, inspecting it. It's been moved since we were here last, closer to the shore. We only have to drag it a few feet.

We take off our shoes. Grace grabs one side of the raft and I grab the other. We pull. It's heavier than it looks and it digs into the gravel. But, inch by inch, it moves.

We shove it into the water, wading up to our knees. "It's freezing!" I gasp.

"There are glaciers that feed into this lake," Grace says. "Hang onto the raft so it doesn't get away. I'll go back for the pole."

Grace gets the pole and lays it across the raft. We climb on, shrieking as the raft tips back and forth. We kneel, clinging with our hands to the edges of the boards like crabs. The raft sinks a tiny bit and icy water splashes over our legs.

"We'll use the pole to keep us from going out," Grace

says. She sticks one end into the water and grunts as she pushes. The raft spins.

"You're making us go deeper!" I say. "You're doing it wrong."

"Then you try," Grace says.

We glower at each other and then we start to giggle. At that moment I think, this is *perfect*. I love this crazy adventure with my sister.

I get the hang of the pole pretty fast. I use it to push us along the shore. As long as you don't mind getting wet, the raft works great. Even Grace admits that. "We should build our own raft," she says.

The wind picks up and little waves bump against the side of the raft. I push the pole down, trying to turn us around.

The pole slips a bit and I try again, leaning into it. I almost tumble off.

The next time I push, I can't feel bottom.

"We're going out!" Grace says.

I jab the pole down, as far as I can, but it won't reach. The raft is bobbing deeper and deeper.

"Bring us in!" Grace yells.

"I'm trying!" I scream.

The water is way choppier out here. It's too deep. The pole is useless. I feel sick. This is all my fault. I lay the pole across the boards and grab on tight.

"What are you doing?" Grace cries.

"We're way too deep," I gasp. "The pole won't reach."

A wave splashes over our legs. The raft is bucking like a wild horse. The wet boards are slippery. It's hard to stay on.

We're blowing farther and farther away from shore.

"We better jump off," I say. "We'll have to let the raft go."

Grace's face turns dead white.

"I don't know how to swim," she says.

I stare at Grace. I've never met a kid who can't swim. "What?"

"I can't swim." Grace sounds terrified. "Not really. I can dog paddle a tiny bit, but my leg drags me down. I don't like it. So I've just never learned."

"Are you kidding me? You can't swim?" I'm horrified. "*Now* you tell me?"

Another wave washes over the raft. My stomach lurches. I can't believe how far away the shore looks already.

There's a screeching sound – it's nails popping out of the wood! Three boards at Grace's end of the raft break loose.

She screams.

She scrabbles towards me on her tummy, her fingers trying to get a grip. I grab her arm.

The raft tilts. Another board comes partly loose, hanging by only one nail, and twisting in the choppy water.

And then one of the logs rolls away.

"It's falling apart!" Grace shrieks.

We're lowered into icy water up to our waists. More boards break off. We cling to the log that's left. It's slippery and hard to hang on to.

We lie with our stomachs across the log, gripping the edge of a board, our legs dangling in the water.

"Kick!" I say. "We'll try to push it in."

We kick hard. But what's left of the raft is mostly under water now and too heavy. We can't make it move.

"I can't kick anymore," Grace says.

I measure the distance to the shore with my eyes. I can make that. I know I can.

But Grace can't.

"I'm going to swim to shore," I say. "I'm going to get help."

Grace is silent.

I take a big breath.

"You've got to hang on," I say.

"I will," Grace says. She sounds scared. But she also sounds very, very brave.

• • • • •

Every time I put my head up for a breath, a wave splashes into my mouth. My arms and legs aren't working properly. They're numb with the cold. It's hard to keep straight. The waves keep pushing me sideways.

I count my strokes. When I get to one hundred, I start over again. I pretend I'm in a race and the crowd is cheering me on.

The next wave shoots water up my nose too. I choke and sputter and my nose burns. *I can't do this.*

Then I think about Grace. If she can be brave, I can be brave too.

My arms feel like wood, but I force them to move.

Stroke, stroke, stroke.

When my feet can finally touch the bottom, I stand up. I bend over at my waist and suck in air. Then, my heart pounding, I look out at the lake.

For a second, I only see gray water and my breath catches in my throat. At last, I spot Grace, bobbing up and down in the whitecaps.

I wave my arms over my head. I pray that she sees me.

I gaze around wildly. The beach and walkway are deserted. There's no one to help me. No one.

I break into a run. The gravel stings my bare feet. But I keep running. I run all the way to the Top Notch Café. The *closed* sign is on the door.

I burst inside. Mom and Daphne are sitting at a table, drinking coffee.

"Grace is drowning!" I scream.

Chapter Thirty

My mom can run like the wind. I never knew that about her before. By the time we get to the beach, I have a stitch in my side and I can barely breathe.

Grace is still clinging to the wrecked raft. She looks tiny in the wild gray water, and so far away. Mom doesn't hesitate for even a second. "Stay right here," she says. "I'm serious, Hope. Don't move." Then she plunges into the lake. She plows through the waves, heading straight towards Grace.

"She's coming, Grace!" I scream, even though I know she can't hear me. "Mom's coming!"

I jump up and down, shivering like crazy.

Soon all I can see are Mom's arms, dipping in and out

of the choppy water. Sometimes I can't even see that. I'm terrified that Mom won't get there in time.

But she does. Her dark head pops up beside Grace. My breath comes out with a whoosh and my legs turn to jelly.

At first, it looks like Mom and Grace are swimming back together. But when they get closer, I can see that Grace is hanging onto the end of one of the boards from the raft and Mom is towing her.

By now a few other people have gathered at the edge of the lake, a man with a dog, a jogger, two girls with bicycles, and Daphne, red-faced and puffing. Everyone is silent, watching.

Mom and Grace reach shallow water. Mom helps Grace stand up and they stumble out of the lake. Mom's arm is wrapped tightly around Grace's shoulders.

"Hallelujah!" cries the man with the dog. Everybody claps.

A shiver runs up my back. I feel so proud of Mom. She is like a heroine in a book.

But I also feel scared. Grace's face is gray, her lips blue. She is shaking from head to toe. She bends over and throws up on the beach.

Then she bursts into tears.

"I want Aunty Eve," she sobs.

· · · · ·

Aunty Eve is standing on the porch, gazing out on the street when we get to Grace's house. We must look crazy, all of us in wet clothes, Mom and Grace still dripping. Aunty Eve stares at us, her face draining of color. "Where on earth have you been?" she cries.

Grace kind of collapses onto Aunty Eve. Aunty Eve folds her into a huge hug. I can tell that she doesn't care one wit that Grace is soaking the front of her dress. By now, Grace is crying really hard. Her shoulders are heaving. Aunty Eve strokes her hair and says, "It's okay, Gracie. You're okay."

"The raft," Grace chokes. "It got too deep…"

"Hush now," Aunty Eve says. "You can tell me everything in a minute. Just be still right now. Take a big breath."

It hits me then, something that I've been missing all along.

Aunty Eve loves Grace.

I think Mom sees it too. She's watching them and her face is all mixed up with sadness and relief.

All of a sudden, I'm shivering like a leaf. Tears well up in the backs of my eyes.

"I think we should go," Mom whispers. She takes my hand and squeezes it.

I bet Aunty Eve and Grace don't even know that we've left.

•••••

Mr. Pinn wants to take Mom and me to a hospital.

"We're not sick," Mom says. "Just cold."

We spend hours in the hot indoor pool, letting the heat soak into our bones.

Healing.

We talk about a lot of things. We talk about the raft and how it wasn't my fault that we got too deep, even though I was in charge of the pole. We talk about how proud Mom is of me for the courage it took to swim to shore for help (as long as I know that I must never do something that dangerous again!). We talk about how much we miss Granny, and even cranky Jingle; and how Mom's secret dream is to work in a florist shop; and how grade six is going to be a brand-new year and a fresh start. We talk about how Mom has never forgiven herself for giving up Grace.

I show Mom my tuck turns and she says that one day she might be watching me in the Olympics.

When we're drying ourselves off with towels, Mom says, "We'll go home tomorrow morning. Mr. Pinn is going to drive us."

Tomorrow? A stupid lump forms in my throat.

The saddest part is that Grace will never know that it was her mother who saved her life.

Chapter Thirty-One

Mom and I are sitting by the fireplace in the lounge when Aunty Eve walks in. She scans the room, spots us and strides over.

"I want to thank you for what you did," she says to Mom. "Grace told me the whole story. You put your own life in danger."

"I'm just so glad she's okay," Mom says softly. "That's all that matters."

"Is it all right if I sit for a minute?"

"Of course," Mom murmurs.

Aunty Eve settles beside us in an armchair. She folds her large brown hands in her lap.

"I know who you are," she says calmly.

I gasp.

Aunty Eve smiles at me. "The first time I saw you, Hope, I wondered. I knew Grace had a twin sister who lived in Vancouver. And then I told myself it was too much of a coincidence."

I'm too stunned to say a word.

"When did you figure it out?" Mom asks. She looks as surprised as me.

"When Hope was helping me with the pies," Aunty Eve says. "I was sure then. You see, Grace and Hope are like two peas in a pod."

I swallow. "We are?"

"Oh yes."

"But...Grace is, well, prettier than me. And she hates jawbreakers, and she likes butterscotch ice cream, and she has best friends, and she doesn't like to read and...and... her feet are much nicer!"

Aunty Eve and Mom burst out laughing.

"When you laugh," Aunty Eve says, "the tips of your noses turn pink. And when you're concentrating on piecrusts, you tilt your heads in exactly the same way! And there's definitely a certain expression in your eyes that I can't describe, but it's there. There's something, just *something*, about you that says twins!"

"That's amazing!" Mom says. She's crying now. At the

same time, she looks like she wants to hug Aunty Eve.

"I asked Grace what your last name was, Hope," Aunty Eve says. "She said King. Then I knew I was right. I've been sending photographs of Grace to a Mrs. King in Vancouver for eight years."

"My mother," Mom says.

"You didn't come to Harrison by accident," Aunty Eve says. "You came to find Grace." She says this, not like a question, but like something she knows is true.

"It was the photographer's stamp on the back of the photographs that told us where she was," Mom explains. "It said Harrison Hot Springs. Hope noticed that."

"So that was it," Aunty Eve says.

I am trying to soak this in. Aunty Eve knew all along. "Does Grace know?" I ask.

"No." Aunty Eve hesitates. "Grace's parents, her *adoptive* parents, were killed in a car accident. I expect you know that."

Mom wipes her tears away. "Yes," she says, "Yes, I do."

"Her father died at the scene. But Sharon lived a few days in the hospital. I stayed by her side. Sharon didn't really have any other family that mattered except for me. I told Sharon I would look after Grace. She made me promise not to tell Grace she was adopted until she was sixteen."

Aunty Eve squeezes her hands together. "It was a

promise that has been hard to keep. I don't believe in keeping secrets from children. Especially that kind of secret. I've always felt Grace has the right to know. But there you are. I promised Sharon. So Grace has no idea that she has a mother and a twin sister."

"I didn't know about Grace, either," I said. "I found out when the picture came in the mail to Granny after she died."

"Your granny died? Oh, I am sorry. Sending the photographs to your grandmother was another promise I made Sharon." She turns to Mom. "Sharon told me you didn't know about the photographs. Another secret."

"What happens now?" I ask.

"Everything's changed," Aunty Eve says. "I'd like to tell Grace. Sharon would understand." She leans forward and touches Mom on the arm. "I'd like to tell Grace before you leave. Just in case she..." Aunty Eve hesitates. "If you agree."

"Yes," Mom says. Her voice is shaking.

"Of course, it might take Grace some time..."

"I understand," Mom says.

Aunty Eve has a brown handbag with her. She reaches in and takes out a piece of paper and a pen and writes something. "My phone number," she says, giving it to Mom. "We'll talk. Lots. There's so much to say. But right now I want to get back to Grace."

She stands up. She leans over and hugs me, and then Mom. She smells faintly of lavender oil. It's a nice smell.

"Thank you," Mom whispers. "Thank you for everything."

• • • • •

After supper, Mom and Mr. Pinn go for a walk. I pack my bag so I'll be ready to leave in the morning. The last thing to go in is my stack of Dear Grace letters.

I sit on the edge of the bed and read them. Every single one. It feels like I'm reading about someone else. Not me. I feel different since I met Grace. I'm not sure how, but it's something I want to think about.

Then I get an idea. I don't know if it's a good idea or a terrible idea. But I know that I'm going to do it.

I find a paper bag from Inkman's in the wastebasket. I scoop up all the letters and put them inside. Then I dash out of the hotel before I can change my mind.

• • • • •

Aunty Eve opens the door when I knock.

"Hope," she says.

It might be my imagination, but I think she looks worried.

"I've brought something for Grace." I give Aunty Eve the paper bag of letters.

"I'll make sure that she gets this," Aunty Eve says.

Aunty Eve doesn't ask me to come in. I'm not sure what to do next.

"Is Grace okay?"

"Of course. She's just resting." Aunty Eve sighs. "Hope, this just isn't the best time. Maybe – "

There's movement behind Aunty Eve, at the end of the hallway. It's Grace, in a blue dressing gown and fuzzy pink slippers. When she gets to the door, I can see that her eyes are red and swollen like she has been crying tons.

"What are you doing here?" she says furiously.

"I – "

"Get out of my house. I mean it."

"Grace," Aunty Eve says.

Grace's eyes blaze. "You're a liar!"

"I didn't lie. I – "

"You can lie by *not* saying things too," Grace spits out. "Was this supposed to be some kind of joke? Ha ha, let's fool Grace!"

"No," I whisper miserably.

"All this time you were pretending to be my friend."

"It wasn't pretend."

"How could you do that to me? Get out of here! Now! I don't ever want to see you again."

I feel like I have been kicked in the stomach. It's hard to breathe.

"*GO!*" Grace screams.

I am such a coward. I turn and run.

Chapter Thirty-Two

I cry myself to sleep, my face mushed into my pillow so Mom won't hear.

In the morning, Mr. Pinn takes the car to gas up and check the tires. Mom goes to the Top Notch to have one last cup of coffee with Daphne.

I can't eat anything and I don't want to talk to anybody. I leave my suitcase in the lobby and go outside. I sit on a bench and stare at the lake.

How did everything go so wrong?

My eyes fill with tears. I open them wide and force the tears back. I don't want to cry anymore. I'm sick of crying. And I'm very, very tired. I guess I just want to go home.

Someone sits down beside me.

I stare at ten bright red toes and then look up. It's Grace.

"You wrote all those letters?" she says. "Are you crazier than I thought?"

I open my mouth to protest. But I can't think of anything to say.

"You're nuts," Grace says. But she's grinning and I feel myself start to smile too. "Cuckoo."

"Did you read them all?" I say.

"Yup," Grace says. "And you know how much I like to read! It took me a gazillion hours."

I snort.

"Why did you do it?" Grace says.

I take a breath. No more secrets. "I don't have a lot of friends," I say. "Well, actually I don't have any friends. So instead I write to you. It helps."

"But Aunty Eve says you just found out about me. But you've got letters from years ago."

"I made you up," I say. "That's what I thought. I started the letters in grade two as soon as I learned how to write. And then I found out you were real and now I think that part of me must have remembered you all along."

It does sound crazy. I can't help it. I start to giggle.

Soon we're both giggling.

Grace takes a breath and says, "I tried last night. To

remember. I tried really hard. But I don't remember. It's so weird."

"Really, really weird," I agree.

"You wrote me all those letters," Grace says.

"Yeah," I say.

We're silent for a moment.

"David came over last night," Grace says. "He wanted to know what happened to his raft. When I told him I almost drowned, he was very nice about it. He says he forgives us."

"That's good," I say. I don't want Grace to get into any more trouble.

"So I told him I forgive him for all the mean things he's said to me. And he invited you and me to a picnic that his family's putting on for his birthday. It's on Saturday and it's going to be a corn roast at Green Point Park."

I've just found out something else that's different between Grace and me. She gets mad fast, but she also forgives fast. Not like me. Granny always said that I could stew over something forever, like a dog with a bone.

Then I realize that Grace said that David invited both of us.

"I won't be here," I say. "We're leaving in a few minutes."

"Maybe," Grace says. "And maybe not."

She sounds all mysterious. "What do you mean?" I say.

Grace's blue eyes sparkle. "Aunty Eve says that if it's

okay with your mom, you can stay with us for awhile. If it works out, even 'til the end of summer. That's three more whole weeks. That is, if you want to."

"If I want to?" I screech. "Are you kidding? Of course I want to!"

Grace jumps up. "Let's go ask your mom."

On the way to the Top Notch, Grace says, "There's just one thing. I'm not sure if I can call your mother *Mom*. I mean, I had another mother and she still feels like my real mom. And I can't call your mother Mrs. King." For the first time, Grace sounds a little unsure.

"Call her Flora," I say promptly.

I spot Mom through the cafe window. She's laughing at something Daphne said. I wave, and she waves back.

"Flora." Grace tries it out. "Do you think she'll mind?"

"Not one bit," I say.

Dear Grace,

I can't believe summer is over. Back to school! Boo hoo! I had the BEST BEST BEST time ever at your place. These are the things I will never forget:

1. Going to the Aga and seeing *My Friend Flicka*. I still say you cried more than me.

2. Hanging out with Louise and Janey, who were so nice to me.

3. The corn roast at Green Point (I'll be forever grateful that David let me borrow so many of his books).

4. The pajama party in the tent in Louise's backyard (I was SCARED STIFF when the boys raided us).

5. The Egyptian hair removal gunk that DIDN'T WORK.

6. FINALLY seeing Fred with the missing ear up close, which was very interesting, but not amazing.

I have made a friend in grade six and her name is Mary. I told her about us and she said it is just like something in a book!!!! So far we have had two overnights, one at her place and one at mine.

Mr. Pinn took me out for a float. He asked

my permission to ask Mom to marry him!!!! He said he fell for her like a ton of bricks when he saw her at Granny's service. I told him that it is okay by me. Mom said yes. The wedding will be next summer. Mom wants you and me to be her bridesmaids.

Mr. Pinn helped me paint Granny's bedroom sunshine yellow. I have a brand new bed, so now I have a bedroom!

Guess what? Mom got a job at a florist shop. Mr. Pinn goes around all the time saying, "Flora sells flowers at a florist shop," which was funny the first time, but is now annoying.

Say hi to Louise and Janey! Tell Aunty Eve thank you for inviting us for Thanksgiving. We can't wait!!

Your sister,
Hope

I stick the letter in an envelope, and get a stamp from Granny's desk. I write Grace's address on it, and put a heart in each corner. I can't believe it! I'm finally sending a real letter to my best friend. I race all the way to the mailbox.

Acknowledgments

I would like to give a huge thanks to Bev Kennedy, who shared her wonderful memories of growing up in Harrison Hot Springs, and to Judy Pickard who made me feel so welcome at the Agassiz-Harrison Museum. It was a pleasure working with the terrific staff at Second Story Press. A heartfelt thank you to my editor, Gena Gorrell, whose attention to the important details made the story so much better.

About the Author

Becky Citra is a former teacher and the author of nineteen books for children. She lives on a ranch in British Columbia where she loves to ride horses, hike, snowshoe, and cross-country ski.